MAI TAI MASSACRE

Charlotte Gibson Mysteries

Book 8

JASMINE WEBB

Chapter 1

I SAT DOWN AT THE TABLE ACROSS FROM ONE OF THE worst men I would ever meet and flashed him a flirty smile.

"Hi, I'm Emma," I lied smoothly. "It's so nice to meet you."

Bigger lie.

In front of me, Connor Howell's face spread into a cocky grin. He was splayed out across the chair, manspreading so much his feet were planted on either side of the table legs. His long-ish dark blond hair was combed back in a look that obviously meant he wanted to give off Chris Hemsworth vibes. His flashy Hawaiian shirt was undone, revealing a strip of slightly burned skin that he puffed out slightly, like one of those birds who pushes out their chest as some sort of mating ritual.

Speaking of birds, the strip of skin in question was dotted with a few strands of hair, reminding me of those failed pigeon nests consisting of four threads and a couple of sticks.

"Hey, Em. Nice to meet you. Connor."

I picked up the drink menu and nervously flipped through the pages, trying to do my best impression of a woman meeting a new guy on a first date.

"Oh, don't worry about that," Connor said, grabbing at the menu and snatching the menu out of my hands. "I know what women want."

The suggestive wink that followed was so bad it took every ounce of willpower I had not to stab him in the eye with the knife next to me.

"How can I say no to that?" I replied, my voice dripping with false honey.

When our server came by a few seconds later, Connor ordered a Budweiser for himself and a vodka with Diet Coke for me.

A red wine would have probably been more fitting, to go with all the flags Connor was throwing up. I'd been here less than a minute, and I already wanted to set this guy on fire.

"So, what are you doing on the island?" I asked when she left, glancing at the menu.

"Oh, you know, just relaxing," Connor replied. "Taking a break from life. I'm from Chicago, and winters there can be rough."

"I've heard. What do you do for work?"

"I'm in finance," Connor replied. "Algorithms. Dealing with millions of dollars on a daily basis.

You know. That sort of thing. Lots of real complex stuff."

"Wow. I bet. That's so interesting," I lied. This guy was *totally* going to try to explain Excel sheets to me before the night was out.

"I was supposed to be in the NHL right now. I played hockey growing up, and I was good."

"Let me guess, a knee injury ended your career?" I asked.

Connor looked surprised. "How did you know?"

I shrugged casually. "Just lucky. I figured a guy like you, obviously headed to the NHL—it wouldn't be that you gave up your career willingly. And injuries are pretty common in hockey, right?"

"They are. It's a tough game. Toughest on earth. I was the top scorer on my team junior year, but a guy slewfooted me three months before the draft, and there went any chance I had. But it's all good. I'm hashtag blessed and all, you know?"

Yes, he really did say "hashtag blessed."

"You must be to work in finance."

"It's the most important job in the country. I work hard, but I play hard. You know what I mean?"

"Like coming here to Hawaii."

Play hard, indeed. I'd found out about Connor two days ago. I'd been hired by a local woman to follow her boyfriend and see if he was cheating on her. Spoiler alert: he was. And I had the audio of what was going on between him and someone else in the bar bathroom to prove it.

But while I was spying on the now-dumped boyfriend, another couple caught my eye. A woman sitting with a guy. She looked fine at the beginning of the night, but as things progressed, she was obviously low-key trying to get away from him, and he wasn't having any of it.

Warning bells had been going off in my brain, and I told the bartender what I suspected. She jumped into action and had one of the other staff members take the woman home herself, despite the man's complaints that she was his date and that he'd paid for everything and deserved the chance to get some.

When I spoke to Jake about it the next day, he said that there was no case. The man hadn't technically committed any crimes, and while Jake agreed with me that he thought the guy was a piece of crap, there wasn't even a complaining witness. He was sympathetic, but he had to work within the confines of the legal system, he explained.

And that was when I decided to give the legal system exactly what it wanted. It didn't take long for me to get the man's name from the bartender—the moron had ended up paying the tab with a credit card after his date left—and with some help from Dorothy, we quickly found his profile on a couple of dating apps.

One catfishing account and some terrible flirting

(on his part) later, here we were. Connor was a predator, and I was a lion dressed up as an antelope.

I wasn't about to wait for a crime to be committed against an innocent person before this guy went to jail.

If the legal system wanted proof, they were going to get it.

"So, how long have you been on the island?" I asked, even though I already knew the answer.

"Four days. I'm here for another week. If I get some sun now, that'll give me the will to keep going until all the snow melts back home. I love it here. You must walk around in bikinis all day. It's so hot."

"Yeah, that's definitely what I do. All day, every day," I said, trying to keep my hatred for this guy from coming out in my tone of voice.

The server returned then with our drinks and asked for our orders.

"Mango BBQ pork ribs for me," Connor said. "But fries instead of macaroni salad. Why do you guys gotta eat macaroni salad with everything? Shit's gross."

The server's smile never dropped even a millimeter as she answered, "Yes, we can do that."

"And I'll have the teriyaki chicken plate," I said, closing the menu and handing it to her. "*With* the macaroni salad."

Connor frowned. "Doesn't that also come with rice? You don't really need both sides, do you? I mean, come on."

I tried to laugh off the insult and resisted the urge to change my order to the biggest burger they had.

"I'm okay with the rice," I replied. I wanted to push back against Connor just a little bit, on something unimportant. I wanted him to know I wouldn't be a *total* pushover. I needed him to start off thinking I was interested, but he needed to see signs I didn't plan on going home with him.

His mouth pressed into a firm line. "Believe me, you don't need the rice."

"Okay, okay," I said, trying to pass the whole thing off as a joke. "No rice for me."

"I'll put those orders in with the kitchen straight away," the server replied, and I couldn't help but notice her narrowing her eyes behind Connor's back as she walked off.

"I'm going to go to the bathroom real quick," I said, standing up.

"You better not be thinking of leaving right now," Connor replied with a teeth-baring smile. The underlying threat was there, and my nose twitched with anger when I registered it.

But instead, I laughed lightly as if Connor had just made a hilarious joke. "Oh, you. Of course I'll be back."

Because I need to come back to throw your ass in jail, you jack-o'-lantern left out until mid-December.

I flashed Connor a smile and walked past him toward the bathrooms at the back of the restaurant.

That he now had his back to me was perfect. He couldn't see that I wasn't going to the bathroom at all.

The restaurant was largely open to the elements, like so many on Maui. That meant even indoors, plants could thrive, and a baby palm tree near the bar was perfect for hiding behind. I wanted to see what he would do when I was away from the table.

And what I saw made me gasp.

I fumbled with my phone to take video as soon as I saw it. Connor reached into the pocket of his khaki shorts and pulled out a tiny vial. He placed it in his lap, and when his hand emerged once more, he had one of those liquid droppers in his hand. His palm hid most of the dropper from anybody who might happen to look in his direction.

He glanced furtively from side to side for a moment before sliding his hand over my drink and letting a couple of drops fall in.

Connor was trying to drug me.

Okay, this guy was a next-level predator. As far as I knew, he hadn't drugged the woman the other day. But maybe I was wrong. Or maybe he was just stepping it up a notch.

Either way, he was spending tonight in jail. And a lot of nights after that, too, if I had anything to do with it.

Because I had the video going on my phone, I had a perfect shot of Connor spiking my drink. To be safe, though, I wanted to keep the evidence.

I spotted our server by the bar and strode over to her. "Hey, listen," I said quickly. "I'm a private investigator, and the guy I'm with is a predator. He just roofied my drink. I need you to come back to the table when I sit down and say you just realized it was made with regular Coke instead of diet. Take the drink back to the bar, but keep it on hand, okay? I'm going to want to test it later."

The server's eyes widened, but then her face hardened. "Got it. Do you want me to call the police? I knew that guy was a jerk, I just didn't know how to warn you."

"Not yet. I'm going to take care of him. I'll let you know if I need anything else."

"Understood. Good luck, and stay safe."

I flashed the woman a reassuring smile then walked back across the wooden floors to the table I'd shared with Connor.

"Good to see you're back. You see, I'm a nice guy, but some women don't understand that."

"Oh, they don't?"

"No. They want men who are bad for them. Guys like me? We get left out in the cold all the time."

"That's not me," I replied. "Now, why don't you tell me about your job?"

Just then, the server appeared. "I'm really sorry, but the bartender just told me he realized he accidentally made this with regular Coke instead of diet," she said, swiftly removing my glass from the table before Connor could protest. "I'll be right back with what you ordered."

"Actually, I'll have the same beer as he's having, if you don't mind," I said.

"Of course," the woman replied, and she disappeared as quickly as she'd arrived.

Connor spun around as she left, looking as if he wanted to call her back. But he must have realized that demanding I drink that glass in particular would have been a massive red flag, because he eventually turned back to face me. "Should have ordered a Bud Light," he muttered under his breath.

"Well, you know, this is a good restaurant. We shouldn't have to worry about stuff like that on a date like this," I said, forcing a smile on my face. Seriously, this guy thought he was *nice*? It was insane on a million different levels.

"I can't talk too much about my job with you, unfortunately. It's a lot of very technical stuff."

"Right. I bet it's all too complicated for someone like me to understand," I replied, working overtime to keep the sarcasm from slipping into my voice.

Luckily, I was an expert when it came to bad dates. I would have to keep this one going for a bit.

The server returned with my beer, the two glasses between Connor and me now identical. This was exactly what I wanted.

"It's very complicated," Connor said. "And it messes up other aspects of my life too."

"Oh?"

"Once women learn what I do, they're all over me. They want the cash that I earn. I immediately become a target of gold diggers. It's too bad, but it's a sacrifice that I have to make."

"I bet." The women fawned all over him so much he had to resort to drugging them to do what we wanted.

"That's why I'm just after something casual these days. Sure, I'm up for paying for a nice dinner that I get to spend with a pretty lady, but I can't trust anybody more than that. I'm just here for a good time."

"That's got to be kind of sad," I said, trying to appear sympathetic.

"It is, but that's women for you. It's all right, though. I've made my choice, and I have my priorities. My job has to take precedence. But that's why I make it clear from the outset that I'm not looking for anything serious."

"Good, because neither am I."

Connor nodded with satisfaction. "Glad to hear it. We're going to have fun tonight. I'm going to glaze you like a Krispy Kreme donut."

Oh my God. Where did this guy learn to flirt, bad porn videos?

After a couple of minutes, I made an excuse to lean down and check something inside my purse. I spent at least twenty seconds down there, and when

I came back up, I knew Connor would have spiked my beer once more.

I took the glass and pretended to take a sip.

"I didn't pick you to be the beer-drinking type."

I smiled, and this time it was real. "Oh, you know, I'm full of surprises."

It didn't take long before I had the opportunity to swap the two glasses around. The two TVs on either side of the bar were showing the Cubs game, which meant Connor had to spin around to look whenever he wanted an update on the score. When Nico Hoerner was at bat, Connor wanted to watch, and I took advantage of the moment to switch the glasses before Connor drank too much of his.

The server returned with our food soon afterwards, and Connor took a big gulp of his beer.

I ate my teriyaki chicken and macaroni salad while I listened to Connor complain about everyone in his life. As he spoke, I was secure in the knowledge that he was going to jail and that by the time I was done with him, he would be begging for prison.

Chapter 2

Over the course of the meal, it quickly became obvious that sure enough, Connor had drugged the beer that was originally mine. He began slurring his words a bit and moving from side to side slightly in his chair.

"All right, let's get the bill," I said. "This has been nice, but I'll pay for my half, and I won't be seeing you again."

"No," Connor snapped, with more force than I had expected. "I will pay for this dinner. I told you. I make a lot of money."

"Okay," I said, motioning for the server to bring over the check. She did, and Connor reached into his pocket and slammed a platinum Amex card onto the table. The woman gave me an "are you okay?" look, I returned a confident smile, and she ran the order through.

As we got up to leave, Connor followed me. We

were in Ka'anapali, which was still flooded with people despite it being low season. Around the main buildings of the major hotel chains dotting the expansive beach on this part of the island, however, were plenty of high walls and dark corners that were easy to get lost in.

Connor began dragging me toward one of them. "My car is this way. I can take us to it," he slurred, grabbing me by the wrist.

"I don't think you should be driving," I replied.

"Who do you think you are to tell me that, bitch?" Connor replied, his grip on my wrist tightening.

My heart began to race. Even though he was drugged, he was still going to try this.

I pulled out my phone and began recording the conversation. "What are you doing? Let me go," I ordered.

"You whores are all the same. Let a man pay for dinner, then you won't give him anything for it. Not even a blow job."

"Technically, that would make me the opposite of a whore. Not that there's anything wrong with sex work," I replied.

Connor laughed as he stumbled, pulling me with him as his shoulder hit the wall. Now we were in a dark alley behind the hotel where we'd eaten; no one was going to come this way except maybe a worker on a cigarette break. This was where he planned to attack me.

"You would think that. Now, get on your knees and give me what I want."

"No."

"No? Okay, fine. I guess I'll just fuck you up against this wall here."

"No."

"I love it when they resist. It makes it so much more fun."

This was my chance. I leaned in, pushing myself against Connor's disgusting body, pressing him up against the wall, my forearm against his neck.

To keep his balance, he let go of my wrist.

"Me too," I whispered as I reached into my bag, grabbed the Taser that was in it, and jammed the weapon as hard as I could against his dick.

Connor let out a cry as he fell to the ground, spasming, grabbing his groin.

"What the fuck did you do?" he shouted, tears welling up in his eyes.

"I Tased you until you were a no-nut," I replied with a grin, standing over him, holding the Taser up so he could see it. "Now, be a good boy and stay there while I call the cops."

"Good. You fucking Tasered me, you dumb bitch."

"And I'll do it again every time you use that word," I replied calmly, reaching down and pressing the weapon into his crotch once more.

Connor screamed, writhing around on the ground in pain. I knew all too well what he was feeling, and he deserved every single second of agony.

Pulling out my phone, I ended the recording then dialed Jake.

"Hey," I said as soon as I heard him answer. "Would you like an attempted rapist on a silver platter? Because boy, do I have one for you."

Jake organized for a squad car to come straight away and promised he would be there as soon as he could.

I stood guard over Connor, who had started whimpering and crying on the ground. He tried getting up once or twice, but his own drugs he'd unknowingly taken prevented him from getting up.

"It sucks, being drugged, doesn't it?" I asked. "Maybe you'll think twice before doing this again. When they let you out of jail, that is. Give it another decade."

"Why would you do this to me?" Connor wailed.

I pulled out my phone and edited the voice recording, ending it right after Connor's explicit threat to rape me.

"Because you deserve it," I replied simply as the sound of approaching sirens began piercing the night. "Because you're not entitled to women's bodies just because you bought them dinner. Because men like you don't stop because you gain a conscience. You just keep doing it until someone stops you. And that's where I come in. So welcome to Maui. Your stay here is going to be a bit longer than you planned."

THREE OR FOUR MINUTES LATER, THE SIRENS GOT louder, and red and blue lights flashed against the walls of the hotel. The sirens were cut suddenly, and I spotted a couple of uniformed officers and motioned them over.

Connor was on the ground, moaning. He'd given up talking to me and had just started crying, curled up in the fetal position.

"This is him," I said to one of the officers, a woman in her twenties with her long brown hair tied in a braid running down her back. "He drugged both my drinks. One of them is inside with the bartender. The other he drank after I switched the glasses. Didn't stop him from trying to rape me when I came out here, though. I have the recording to prove it."

"Does he need medical attention?" the woman asked while her partner dragged Connor to his feet and cuffed him.

"Maybe, but I don't think he deserves it," I replied, earning myself the slightest hint of a smile from the police officer.

"Put him in the car for now," the woman ordered.

"Don't listen to her," Connor slurred at the cop. "She Tasered me. Why isn't she under arrest?"

The other officer shoved Connor into the squad car and slammed the door shut behind him, cutting off his protestations.

"Take care of her until the detectives get here; I'll go get the drink the bartender saved and take a statement from the staff," the woman said.

She nodded and then turned and walked toward the hotel while I waited for Jake to arrive.

It didn't take long; Jake must have either already been in the north end of Kihei or broken all the speed records known to man to get here. As soon as he arrived, he jumped out of the car and raced over to me while Liam stayed near the car, leaning against it like a fatter, scowlier version of Stay-Puft, the marshmallow dude from *Ghostbusters*.

The flashing red and blue lights against his chiseled cheekbones made Jake look like a model walking out of an ad.

"Are you all right?" he asked.

"I'm fine. Connor isn't, though."

I ran Jake through everything that had happened. When I was finished, he ran a hand through his hair.

"On the bright side, it looks like the bar for what counts as a good date between us is now on the floor," he said.

I laughed. "Oh, man, that bar is in hell."

Jake narrowed his eyes at me. "I just have one question: where did you get a Taser?"

My eyes widened. "Uh, the Taser store?"

A disbelieving scowl crossed Jake's face. "Oh yeah? Which one?"

"Uh, the one in the industrial area behind Kihei. You know, where they also sell guns."

"Where did you really get this? And don't lie to me."

"I can do one or the other, but I can't do both."

Jake pressed the palms of his hands into his eyes. "Charlie, you're impossible." Then, he paused, his face blanching. "Wait, this isn't *my* Taser, is it? The one the police department gave me."

"No, of course not," I replied quickly. "I know you too well; you'd realize it was missing straight away."

My eyes gave me away as they landed on Liam.

"You didn't," Jake gasped as his eyes followed mine.

"He just leaves it in an unlocked drawer. Do you know how dangerous that is?" I replied. "Anyone could have taken it."

"Anyone didn't have to be *you*. Why did you need a Taser anyway? You're basically the only person in the world that I think would be safer with a gun."

"I didn't want to shoot the guy. I just needed to be able to defend myself against him if he tried anything," I replied with a shrug. "Liam can have his Taser back. Not that he really deserves it."

"I can't believe I'm having this conversation," Jake replied.

"You're the one asking questions you didn't want to know the answers to."

"No, I'm asking questions I wished had different answers."

"Po-tay-to, po-tah-to."

"Do you know that stealing a police officer's weapon is a crime?" Jake hissed.

"I didn't steal it. I borrowed it."

"Well, you had better make sure it gets back to his desk and fast. I can't believe you of all people would choose a Taser as a weapon."

"I'm more experienced with it than anyone I know."

"Experience with getting zapped by one is *very* different from experience in using one."

"You taught me how to use it, remember?" I replied smugly.

Jake opened his mouth to retort but closed it again. I grinned as I realized he had nothing to reply with. It was true; Jake had taken me shooting and taught me to use a Taser in the hopes that by knowing how to use it, I might fall victim to one less often.

That part hadn't quite worked out, but it meant I did know how to operate one because of him.

"You're impossible," he finally said.

"I just got a bad dude off the streets."

"I can't deny that. Now, come on. We're going back to the police station. You're going to put the Taser back before Liam realizes it's missing and before Connor has another chance to accuse you of Tasering him and you get found with the weapon on you."

"It's perfectly legal."

"It's legal to carry a Taser. It's *not* legal to possess a stolen Taser, and it's even *less* legal when that Taser belongs to the police."

"That's biased."

Jake just shook his head. "Sometimes I wonder what I did in a past life to deserve you."

"Probably did something amazing that got you a Nobel Peace Prize."

"You're impossible. Do you want me to give you a ride back to Kihei?"

I shook my head. "Thanks, but I don't want to leave Queenie up this side of the island."

"I'll see you soon, then."

I watched Jake as he walked back to his car, my eyes drawn down to his pants.

When he climbed back into the car, I grabbed my things and walked back to Queenie. This was quite enough of excitement for one night.

Chapter 3

I FOLLOWED JAKE BACK ALONG THE HIGHWAY AS WE headed toward Kihei and the police station on that side of the island. When we entered, the receptionist, Andrea, waved me through. She knew me by sight by now.

Jake sat down at his desk, and Liam walked straight over to the vending machine at the other end of the station.

While he spent ten minutes trying to decide between a KitKat bar and a Snickers—he would totally end up buying both, anyway—I slipped the Taser from my purse and casually put it back in the unlocked top drawer of his desk, across from Jake's.

"You have got to be kidding me," Jake muttered. "*That's* where you got it from? I thought you were kidding."

"As I said, it was easy," I replied with a shrug. I was tempted to grab Liam's chair and sit in it, just to annoy him, but changed my mind when I thought about who normally sat in it. The CDC could probably find all-new diseases if they tested the seat.

Instead, I grabbed a plain metal visitor's chair from a nearby desk and sat on it, facing Jake.

"I have to do some paperwork to take this case, since it was in Ka'anapali," he explained.

"Fair enough. It'll be worth it. Free conviction."

"What have you got?"

"Video of him slipping something into my drink. The cops should have the drink in question, because I asked the server to keep it on hand. And I have audio of him threatening me outside. He was out of it but not passed out. I'm guessing either he messed up the dosage, or he didn't want to give me so much that people would obviously notice something was wrong. Or the weight difference between us meant that it didn't affect him as badly as it would have me."

Jake nodded. "I'm glad you're safe. That was a really dangerous thing to do."

"I know. But he was dangerous, and I had to get him off the streets. If it wasn't me, he was going to try it with some other poor innocent woman and ruin her life. At least I knew what I was getting into. And I came prepared."

"You did," Jake replied. "I just wish you hadn't stolen a Taser to do it. When did you even take it?"

I shrugged. "A couple weeks ago. I figured it might come in handy. It was just sitting there."

"You're impossible."

"Your partner is incredibly irresponsible."

"I can't argue with that right now, I suppose. Oh, good, here's an email from the police in Ka'anapali. They've identified the guy."

"Connor Howell," I said. "Twenty-seven, from Chicago. Here on holiday, now an extended one at Club Halawa."

Jake grinned. "Sure is. He was staying at the Sheraton; I'm going to get a warrant to search his room. He had a drug on him. It's being sent to the lab along with the drink the bartender saved. I need the video and audio from you."

"Sure, I'll AirDrop it," I said, pulling out my phone. I sent the files over. "Do you need me for anything else?"

"I think this is it for now. Thanks, Charlie."

I nodded. Jake and I always had a bit of tension when we worked together, more so since the last case. But he hadn't scolded me about doing this—he knew I always would. He asked that I call him first when I did things like this. And I did. He was slowly beginning to trust me professionally, and I was glad for it. I wasn't sure our personal relationship would survive if we couldn't.

I said goodbye to Jake and headed back out to the parking lot. Sitting inside Queenie, I texted Dot and Rosie, letting them know of the successful night we'd just had. Connor was in jail, and thanks to the evidence I provided, it would be a long time before he was ever a free man again.

I was just getting ready to put the Jeep into gear and drive home when suddenly, a half dozen officers ran from the building to their squad cars. I watched on curiously as they all left, sirens and lights blaring, turning onto the highway in the direction of Wailea.

What was going on?

My phone began ringing in my hand just then. It was Marina Clarke, the manager of the Maui Diamond resort in Wailea. I'd done work for her before as a private investigator.

"Hello?" I answered.

"Charlie, I need you down here right away. There's been an explosion. I don't have any details yet. I'm not even sure a crime has been committed, but I want you here just in case. Get any answers you can. If we've been attacked, I'm pulling out all the stops to make sure we find out what's happened."

"I'm on my way," I replied.

As I pulled the Jeep out of the lot, I called Dot and immediately put the phone on speaker.

"Good to hear you've had another successful night," Dot told me.

"Yeah, for now. But there's been an explosion at Maui Diamond. Half the cops in the station are heading there now, and Marina just called me for help."

"A gas leak?" Rosie asked in the background. "Or something more sinister?"

"I'm not sure yet. I don't think Marina knows either. I'm on my way now to see what I can find out."

"I'll look at the chatter online," Dot said.

"I'll meet you down there," Rosie added. "Something like this happening in Maui—it's big. It could have repercussions."

"I agree. I'll see you soon."

I ended the call just as Jake and Liam passed me. They were headed to the crime scene as well. It was all hands on deck. Whatever had happened, it was bad.

The Maui Diamond resort was one of the largest and most expensive on the island, located in Wailea, the part of the island that had been specifically developed as a spot for luxury resorts. A single night in a basic room at the Maui Diamond ran upwards of six hundred dollars a night. In the offseason.

Getting a room here around the Christmas holidays cost more than what I made in a week.

And right now, the resort was in chaos.

The palm trees that lined the drive leading to the resort lobby flashed with emergency vehicle lights. At the entrance, the limousines, Mustangs, and high-end sedans that normally lined the curb had been replaced with fire trucks, ambulances, and police cars.

People were huddled together in small groups around the building, watching as the emergency service personnel moved in and out of the building, moving swiftly with the authority that came from knowing their roles in an emergency and executing them well. Yellow police tape cordoned off the building's entire interior, but I could see smoke pouring out from the corridor down to the left.

A crew of EMTs wheeled a stretcher toward the front door, quickly loading their patient into one of the waiting ambulances before driving off at top speed.

I looked around and saw Rosie standing off to the side, by herself, surveying the scene.

As I made my way toward her, she nodded in greeting when she saw me.

"I haven't seen anybody suspicious yet," she said. "But of course, there's no telling they were even on the scene if this was a bomb. If it were me, I'd have set it up with a timer to avoid being near when it went off."

"Do you think it's a bomb?"

"In my experience, explosions from gas leaks tend to be larger than this one appears to be. Especially in a building of this size. I am not a betting woman, but if I were, I would expect the investigators to find evidence of an explosive device. You haven't spoken to Jake yet."

It was a statement, not a question, but I still shook my head. "He passed me on the way. I imagine he's still in there, getting up to speed. There's no chance we'll be allowed through that line, so let's see what we can find out from people out here."

Rosie and I walked through the crowd, and it didn't take long before we found a woman walking along, shod in a single flip-flop, looking dazed.

She was in her forties, with big blond hair singed with soot. Part of her spaghetti-strapped, pink-and-orange dress had ripped near her calf. A small bag hung limply at her side.

"Excuse me," I called out to her, and the woman turned to look at us, her gaze distant.

"Are you all right?" I asked. "Do you need medical attention? There are plenty of EMTs and doctors around."

The woman shook her head. "No. No, I'm okay. Physically, anyway. I don't know… I just don't know."

"Come over here," Rosie ordered kindly but firmly, leading her toward a bench on the path that led around the back of the resort and toward the water. "You need to sit. Charlie, go find some water."

I nodded and raced to the next resort over. After a quick explanation to the woman at their front lobby, I was immediately given three bottles of water. I raced back over to where I had left Rosie and the other woman.

Rosie was sitting next to her on the bench, holding her hand kindly.

As soon as I returned, I opened the bottle of water for the woman and handed it to her.

She drank a small sip, closing her eyes. Then she took another, bigger sip.

"I can't believe it," she eventually said. "I just can't believe it."

"Do you want to talk about it?" Rosie asked.

The woman nodded. "I need to tell someone. It doesn't feel real."

"What's your name?" Rosie started. "Where are you from?"

"Gabrielle. Gabby. I'm from Billings, Montana."

"Are you here by yourself?"

"For work. I'm with a work group. There's a conference. I was having dinner with my colleagues. We were in the seafood restaurant at the back of the building. Everything was completely normal. Then, all of a sudden, there was an explosion. I was on my back. My ears were ringing. People were screaming and running around. I had no idea what was happening. I got up, and I just... I walked off. I didn't know where. My head hurt. And now I'm here."

"Okay, I think you might have a concussion. We're going to get you some medical help," Rosie said. "Where did the explosion come from?"

"It was nearby. I think it was across from me."

"Where were you seated in relation to the building?"

"We weren't near it. We were by the railing, overlooking the ocean. One of the last things I remember thinking before the explosion was how pretty the water was, even at night. I think it might have come from the table next to us. We were so close."

"Do you know anything about them?" I asked.

The woman in the torn dress shook her head. "No. Not a thing. Sorry."

"Okay. We're going to find you some help," Rosie said. "I'm going to stay with you. Charlie, go find some EMTs."

"Got it," I said. I immediately stood up and headed back to the main lobby.

I explained the situation to a police officer standing guard. Three minutes later, a doctor followed me toward the bench where we'd seated Gabby.

We left them together, and Rosie and I walked along the path toward the beach.

Above, the sound of whirring helicopter blades filled the night air.

"That's the medevac helicopter," Rosie said. "Eurocopter EC135. I recognize the sound of it."

"Of course you do," I replied with a small smile.

Walking along the path, I spotted two news crews already set up on the beach, with the resort in the background. Large spotlights shone on the presenters, who spoke solemnly into their microphones.

"As of yet, we don't know what has caused this explosion at one of Maui's most famous resorts. We'll update you with more information as soon as we have it, but currently, there are more questions than answers. One onlooker we spoke to said they believe it was a bomb, but the authorities are yet to make a statement."

I raised my eyebrows at Rosie. "Well, that's going to cause some ripples around here."

"I agree," she said. "Tourism is the lifeblood of Maui's economy at the moment, for better or for worse. If this wasn't an accident—and it doesn't sound as if it was—then the shit is going to hit the fan on this island."

She wasn't wrong.

Chapter 4

ROSIE AND I STAYED IN THE AREA FOR ANOTHER hour before Marina called me again and asked to meet. We joined her on the path outside the resort.

Wearing a button-up beige shirt and a pair of tailored pants, Marina was dressed fancily by island standards. Her black hair was tied in a tight bun behind her head, and her flat shoes added no height to her short, thin frame.

As soon as she reached us, she held out a hand for me to shake. "Charlie, it is nice to see you again, although not under these circumstances."

"You too," I replied as I shook her hand. "This is Rosie, an associate of mine."

Marina shook her hand as well then immediately got down to business. "I've just spoken with the Chief of Police and the Maui County Fire Chief. Given the hard evidence and statements from witnesses, they don't believe this was an accident. A bomb was set off in one of our restaurants, on purpose."

I swallowed hard at the statement, despite having been nearly certain that was the case, given what Gabby had told us. "What do they know?"

"The device, which they believe was set off remotely, was underneath one of the tables at La Mer, our French-inspired seafood restaurant. It's our flagship. The chef is Guillaume Gauthier."

"I've seen his show on the Food Network," I interrupted.

"Yes, you would have. He's one of the top celebrity chefs in the country. We began our collaboration last year. La Mer is one of the most exclusive restaurants on the island. Reservations generally fill months in advance."

"We'll need a list of all of your reservations for today," Rosie said.

"Of course, I can get that for you. However, my one request is that your second priority be discretion. I know you understand this, Charlie, but this case will reflect poorly on this resort. On this whole island. We need it solved as quickly as possible but also while doing everything possible to maintain our reputation."

"Understood. I will tread with care."

Marina motioned to the news crews stationed nearby. "I know all of this is inevitable. I just need answers yesterday so we can show that there is no further threat to the safety of this resort's guests and this island's visitors. You have full access to the resort and its employees, as far as I'm concerned. Anything you need, you call me directly and I will make sure you have it. I've also told the Chief of Police that I've hired outside help and requested that he not do anything to impede your separate investigation."

"Thank you. I do have a few questions for you. First of all, have you or anyone at the hotel received any threats lately?"

"No, nothing of the sort."

"Have any employees, current or former, recently made threats, or been laid off?"

"No. We're coming into the summer high season; we're looking to hire staff right now, not lay off. We did have to fire someone three weeks ago, but I can't imagine he would do this."

"All the same, we'll need his contact information," I said.

"Of course."

"Are there CCTV cameras that cover the restaurant?"

"They cover the interior, yes. The patio has some coverage, but it's not complete. We like to keep some tables free from CCTV footage for the diners' own comfort. We get a lot of celebrities. Frankly, we've never really had a problem that required the security camera footage before."

"Can you please email me all of the footage

you've got for the past week?" I asked. "I'll need to see it myself."

"I'll do that straightaway."

"Do you know what group was at the table the bomb was under?"

"According to my manager, Janice, it was a group from San Francisco. A small team from a drug manufacturing company."

"How many casualties are there?" Rosie asked.

"The last I heard, we had four deaths and twelve hospitalizations," Marina replied quietly. "One of them was a staff member, Emily Hornby. It's awful."

We asked Marina a few more questions, but it quickly became obvious she didn't know much right now.

"All right, we're going to get started on this investigation."

"I don't need to impress on you how important this is," Marina said.

"No," I replied quietly. "You don't."

After saying goodbye, Marina headed back toward the resort entrance, and Rosie and I returned to the parking lot.

"At least we know it was a bomb," I said. "It's not much to go on, but it's a start. Remotely detonated."

"That means it was either set off with a timer, or if our bomb maker wanted to be more specific about the timing, they could have set it up to trigger when they performed an action. These days, it's quite simple for someone who knows what they're doing to set up a bomb to a cell phone trigger. When someone phones the number attached to the bomb, it detonates. It's possible to do that with untraceable burner phones."

"Is it easy to do?"

"That depends. For someone skilled with their hands, with a modicum of knowledge of chemistry and physics? Yes. For anyone else? It depends on how good they are at following instructions they find on the internet."

"So we should assume that anybody we consider a suspect would have the skills to create this bomb."

"That is the most prudent course of action, yes," Rosie agreed.

"Good to know. Okay, let's head over to Dot's place and see what she can find on the CCTV footage."

As I got back to Queenie, I saw Marina had emailed me the information I'd asked for. I forwarded it to Dot, sent her a text letting her know we were coming, then drove off.

When we arrived at Dot's apartment, she had everything Marina had sent me loaded up and ready to go.

"I'm going to do a more in-depth search for the

man who was fired recently," Dot said as we walked in, "but for now I've found some of his social media accounts, most of which are public. We also have the information Marina sent. He worked in customer service and was fired three weeks ago after verbally abusing a customer."

"Yup, that'll do it," I said dryly. "Are there details?"

"According to the customer, they were trying to check in, and asked the man—Dylan, his name is. Dylan Markham—about getting a reservation at La Mer. He told them he couldn't help, that they were fully booked. Reportedly, when the man tried to convince Dylan to help them get a table anyway, Dylan began yelling at them. They complained to management, the tapes were reviewed, and Dylan was let go."

I raised my eyebrows. "Okay, well, I'd love to see that interaction for myself. And talk to Dylan. I might be wrong, but I wouldn't be surprised if he had a very different story to tell about how things went down. Something is weird about that report. He just happened to yell at them over nothing?"

"I agree," Rosie said.

"As someone who has recently worked in a customer service setting, I have to say, people seem to be getting more and more unhinged these days. It's wild the number of people who would yell at me just for telling them that they couldn't have fifty different samples of ice cream and needed to order something for real. Or who would complain that we charged extra for chocolate sauce."

Dot shook her head. "Some people never learned real manners."

"It's okay. I managed. Also, anytime anyone who was rude to me was obviously in their forties or fifties, I would ask them at the checkout counter if they wanted a senior's discount," I said with a grin.

Rosie snorted.

"Getting back to this case, I obviously haven't had a chance to go through all the camera footage, but I've seen the footage from the explosion. The bomb in question was off scamera."

"So either the person who planted it got very lucky, or they knew where the lenses were pointed," Rosie mused.

"That's a *wild* amount of luck," I pointed out. "How much of that patio area is covered?"

"I'd say maybe sixty percent, at a guess," Dot said. "Here. These are all the cameras from the restaurant in the minute leading up to the explosion."

She tapped at the computer keyboard for a couple of seconds, and the computer screens in front of her filled with smaller screens, each showing security camera footage.

The resort had obviously shelled out for a good security system. Rather than blurry, low-resolution video that looked like it was taken with a cell phone from 2002, the shots were crisp, clear, and time-stamped at the bottom. We had no need to pretend we could magically enhance footage like every cop show in the world seemed to do.

There were eight different shots taken from various spots in the restaurant. One camera covered most of the back kitchen area. Two cameras took care of the bar near the entrance. Another three covered the rest of the restaurant's covered interior, which opened seamlessly onto a large patio leading out to the beach, with large tile columns between the open spaces.

Those cameras covered most of the patio, but as Marina had pointed out, there were a few blind spots.

The restaurant itself was immaculate. Warm, wooden flooring covered the space, with can lighting in the ceiling supplementing the glow from the hanging fancy rattan chandeliers. Next to the entrance lay a long bar, the far side of which contained an exposed shelf displaying fresh fish, the day's catch that was presumably to be cooked in the kitchen later. Tables draped with white cloth were contrasted with dark wooden chairs, and from each table came the muted glow of a candle holder.

"The explosion takes place at nine seventeen," Dot explained.

I immediately gazed at the timestamp; she had the video set up two minutes earlier. My eyes moved between all the camera views as Dot pressed Play.

Servers bearing trays laden with glasses and drinks moved expertly between the tables.

Diners ate and drank, some quietly conversing among themselves, while others were obviously slightly rowdier. That much was obvious even though the security camera footage had no audio. Nothing stood out to me as extraordinary, and as the timestamp at the bottom ticked closer to nine seventeen, I found myself strumming my fingers nervously against my thighs.

Then, it happened. Suddenly, the entire scene was turned upside down. The screen from one of the outdoor cameras went completely white for a couple of seconds. The shots from the interior cameras showed people in a state of surprise but mostly directly unaffected.

However, the exterior cameras were another story. People immediately ran in every direction. Some ran toward what was obviously the scene, and a few took out their phones, calling what I assumed were emergency services.

A palm tree just barely in view of one camera had caught on fire. A few seconds later, one of the servers rushed onto the scene armed with a fire extinguisher and coated the fire with white foam.

There were injured people all around the scene. I was struck by how quickly those unaffected came to the aid of those who clearly needed help. Although some people fled immediately, most stayed behind.

The destruction and devastation made a somber scene, and the three of us watched in silence for a few minutes before Dot pressed Pause.

"There you have it," she said. "Unfortunately, the blast site itself wasn't in view."

"Going by the angles, and from what we can see, I believe it was just to the left of what's visible in camera six," Rosie said.

"Yes," Dot agreed. "I think you're right."

"Did anybody see anything suspicious?" I asked. "I didn't. Everything seemed pretty normal until the explosion."

"I didn't," Dot replied.

"Nor me," Rosie added.

"Okay, we all have copies of this footage, since I've sent it to Rosie. And it's getting late. Why don't we call it a night and meet up again tomorrow, once everyone's had a chance to look at it individually. You never know what we'll find if we're looking separately," Dot suggested.

"We meet back here tomorrow morning, then," Rosie said.

"I'm going to go up to the hospital and see what I can find out," I said. "There might be people there I can talk to, who know what went on."

"Good idea," Rosie agreed.

The three of us split up, and I headed back to the highway and toward Kahului, home to the hospital on Maui.

Chapter 5

Iᴛ ᴡᴀs ᴊᴜsᴛ ᴀꜰᴛᴇʀ ᴇʟᴇᴠᴇɴ ᴏ'ᴄʟᴏᴄᴋ ᴏɴ ᴀ Thursday, but the emergency room was packed with people. Instinctively, I looked outside to see if the moon was full. Zoe, my best friend and emergency room doctor here at the hospital, was a proponent of the idea that at the full moon, everything in healthcare somehow got a little bit crazier than usual.

I couldn't see it in the night sky, so I went inside and had a look around. Almost all the chairs were full. Some people had obviously come from the resort in Wailea. They were the ones with burns and scratches, their clothes covered in soot. Others simply had bad timing on top of bad luck with their emergencies. In one of the chairs sat a man in his thirties, on his phone, his face covered in black soot, a tear in his shirt. I made my way to him and sat down.

"Hi," I said.

He didn't even bother looking up from his phone. "No comment."

"I'm not a reporter," I said.

My reply got him to at least tear his eyes from his screen and look at me. "You look like a reporter. Who are you?"

"Charlotte Gibson, private investigator. I'm looking into the bombing at the resort on behalf of the manager."

"He doesn't trust the police to do it?"

"She does, but she's willing to go further and hire whoever she needs to in order to find the person who did this."

"Shit, I recognize you. You're that investigator involved in the Marion Hennessey thing."

"That's me. Now, can you tell me what happened? Where were you seated at the restaurant?"

"I think our table was where the bomb was planted," the man said, rubbing the back of his head and squeezing his eyes shut. "Everything was normal. We were all having a nice dinner. Then, the next thing I know, I'm lying on my back, the wind's been knocked out of me, and people everywhere are screaming. A tree was on fire. I drove myself here. I'm waiting to see a doctor, but I expect it's going to take a while. There are people worse off than me right now."

"You're hurt?"

The man pulled his torn shirt up, wincing as he did so, to reveal a large gash in his side. "Just this. It's not deep, and it's not bleeding much. Believe me, I'm happy to wait. I'm not going to die anytime soon."

"You were at the table where the bomb went off? Who was with you?"

"There were nine of us. We're a team from a biotech company based out of San Francisco. We just completed a major project we'd been working on for a couple of years, and this trip was to celebrate that."

"All of you work for that same company?"

"Well, no. Five of us are on the team, and we were all able to bring a plus-one. There are two spouses, a friend, and a sister. My wife was supposed to come, but she had a last-minute emergency at work and couldn't take the time off. I was upset for her, since she's always wanted to visit Hawaii, but in the end, I'm so glad. I don't even want to think about what it would be like if she were here. We're supposed to fly back to California tomorrow. This was our last night out, and we all got together to celebrate it. I don't even know what we're going to do now…"

His voice trailed off.

"What's your name?" I asked.

"Ed."

"Did you notice anything strange at the restaurant tonight, Ed? Anything you can think of that was out of the ordinary? Someone who didn't belong?"

He thought for a bit but then shook his head. "No. I really can't. Everything seemed fine. I showed up around seven, as we'd planned, and the host took me to the table. Courtney was already there, with her husband, Aiden. And so was Russel and his friend Amir. So I joined them; I was sitting next to Courtney. She's in surgery, the last I heard. So is Amir. Aiden and Russel I haven't heard."

"So you were the fifth to arrive," I confirmed.

"That's right. About ten minutes later, Larry and his wife Lara showed up then Howard and his wife Julia. That made the entire group. We had drinks, we ordered appetizers, and we were just settling in with our mains when it happened."

"Is there any reason to think anyone had something against your group, or a specific member of your group?" I asked.

Ed looked at me incredulously. "Are you serious? No, of course not. This had to be a random thing. Wrong place, wrong time. Who would attack us?"

"I'm not saying that's what happened, but right now, early in the investigation, I need to pursue all lines of inquiry."

Ed rubbed a hand down his face. "Okay. Okay, yeah, I get that. But I'm telling you, you're on the wrong track. Who would come after us? And we were in Hawaii. No one in our group knows anybody here. How could we have problems with someone?"

"The job you do, can you tell me about it?"

"It's all very hush-hush," Ed said.

"I'm not looking to steal your company's secrets, Ed. I got a D in biology in high school. I'm just trying to find out what happened, and this might be important."

"Look, I can tell you this: Our project involved finding a new molecule that can guide cells to produce proteins that are trained to kill invasive or malignant cells. It's a major development that could have a ripple effect through the entire medical community."

"Malignant cells… You mean cancer?" I asked.

"Potentially, yes. Obviously, it's very early days. There are still years and years of finalizing and testing and FDA approval ahead of us before this comes anywhere near the market. But if we get there—and it is a big if—this could revolutionize not only cancer treatment but all kinds of medical treatments. If we can work with this molecule in question, we could teach it to do the same with viruses. Bacteria. It could be a catch-all to train the body to reject foreign intruders. But we're still a long way from that. We're going to apply for expedited approval, but it will take a long time."

"But you have found the molecule in question?"

"Yes. That's what our team is celebrating here

this week. And it's turned into a complete disaster. I can't believe it."

"Is there anyone out there, or any companies, who would want to see this stopped from going onto the market?"

"Sure. Our competitors. I'm not privy to that kind of information, but I'd be shocked if ten or fifteen other biotech companies weren't out there trying to figure out what we just did. It's a race to the patent office with this sort of thing. But that's how this industry has been for decades. It's very rare that anyone is killed over pharmaceutical industry competition. There was the unsolved murder of that Canadian couple a few years back. The founder of Apotex. And because no one knows who killed them, we don't even know if it's anything linked to the job."

"So you don't think it could have been a competitor coming after you?"

"No, that's ridiculous," Ed said. "It would be so outside the realm of possibility, I can't believe it would happen."

"There would be billions of dollars at stake here, though, wouldn't there?" I asked.

"Without question. But still. We're scientists, not psychopaths."

"Ted Kaczynski was a scientist," I pointed out.

Ed had no reply to that.

"But okay," I continued. "Let's say you're right and that this had nothing to do with your work.

What about the individual people? Do you know of any problems they were having? Any problems *you* were having?"

Ed shook his head. "No. Nothing to this extent. I mean, everyone has problems. But they're little things. Howard is involved in a dispute with his insurance company over a car accident from a month ago. They don't want to pay to fix his bumper. Amir was complaining that he's probably going to get laid off at work next month, despite his company posting record profits. That sort of thing. Courtney's husband is a bit weird, and I don't really get why she stays with him. But it's not something you kill someone over. And with a *bomb*?"

"Okay, got it. Why do you think the husband is weird?"

Ed shrugged. "It's nothing, really. Like in the whole scheme of things. It wouldn't have had anything to do with this, but he's one of those guys with a superiority complex, you know? Always correcting Courtney in public. Acts like he won thirty games in a row on *Jeopardy!* You know the type. We would make plans for dinner, and he'd ask if they had a trivia night. He's just a know-it-all douchebag. Also, he's a pilot, and he makes sure everyone knows it. He introduces himself that way, and he corrects Courtney if she doesn't call him Captain."

I raised my eyebrows. "Seriously? He makes his wife call him Captain?"

Ed tried to laugh then winced and grabbed at his side. "Yeah. It's really stupid. Courtney rolls her eyes and goes along with it most of the time."

"Sounds like a weirdo."

"He is. But not in an aggressive way at all. That's what I mean; it's not got anything to do with this." Ed leaned in close to me. "Look, I really think this was a random attack. Why would anyone do this to us? And here, in Hawaii? It makes no sense. If someone we knew was trying to kill someone in our group—or the whole group—wouldn't they be better off doing it in California? We have no links to Hawaii. We're just here for a week."

"Got it. Thanks. If you think of anything else, or if any of the other people you were with can talk to me, can you give me a call? Anytime is fine." I pulled out a card and handed it to Ed.

"Sure. Can I take a few, to give to the others?"

I gave him an extra ten or so business cards, and he absentmindedly flipped them around in his hands. "Thanks. I'll make sure everyone talks to you. I want the person who did this found. I don't even know if everyone is…" Ed's voice trailed off.

"I hope they're all okay," I replied, knowing from what Marina told me that at least four of them weren't.

I stood up and went to see the nurse at reception. It was Cora, a tall twentysomething with big blue eyes and long blond hair tied back.

"Hi, Charlie," she said to me with a smile. I

wasn't sure if she recognized me because I was friends with Zoe, or because if this hospital had a frequent-flyer program—or frequently-Tasered—I'd have platinum status.

"Hi," I replied. "The resort hired me to look into the bombing."

Cora shook her head. "I couldn't believe it when they told us. A mass casualty incident, here on the island. We've called in everyone we can, and there's a team being sent in from Honolulu that we hope is arriving in the next twenty minutes. We've got four dead already and a couple who are probably not going to make it. And at least fifty injuries. Some are still in the waiting room."

"It's awful. Look, I need to get all the information I can, especially from anyone who was at that table."

Cora pursed her lips. "You're not going to get any right now. Not from anyone in here, anyway. Three of them were the victims seated at the table. The fourth was a server walking past the table when the bomb went off, from what I understand. And the others are all either in surgery or still unconscious. Sorry, Charlie. Try again in the morning. And even then, I can't guarantee anything. It's going to depend on the patients, their condition, and if they even want to speak to you. But their health is our priority."

"Totally understand, Cora. Thanks. I'll come by

in the morning and see if any of them are available. Good luck here tonight."

"Thanks. We're going to need it."

I headed back out into the night, thinking about what I'd learned from Ed. His analysis of the situation seemed pretty right to me. It felt unlikely that anyone would follow a team from San Francisco all the way to Hawaii just to leave a bomb at the table where they were eating. How could they have found out they would be at that specific table, anyway? The bomb had to have been left before the group were seated; otherwise they surely would have noticed it. Right?

There were so many questions I needed to have answered. I made a mental note of everything I would have to do tomorrow. When I got home, I took Coco for a quick late-night excursion to walk and do her business. Then I opened my laptop and started going over the camera footage once more.

Sleep could wait. Someone had just set off a bomb in Maui. I had to get to the bottom of this.

I immediately pulled out my notepad and silently cursed myself for not asking Ed for a last name. Luckily, by typing in all the first names I'd received along with "biochemistry San Francisco" into Google, I quickly got full names for everybody involved.

Edwin Weaver was a molecular biologist working for Valantir Technology—the kind of company that would totally show up in an "is this a real pharmaceutical company, or the name of an elf from *The Lord of the Rings*" online quiz. I recognized him immediately from the picture on his LinkedIn profile, and from there it didn't take me long to find the others.

Courtney Silva was a senior scientist also working for Valantir Technology. Her professional headshot showed a woman in her forties with sleek light-brown hair and matching eyes standing in a lab coat with her arms crossed in front of her, a confident smile on her face.

Russel McCarthy looked younger, maybe in his late twenties, around my age. He'd graduated from Harvard for his undergrad, masters, and PhD, and was obviously a bit of a prodigy.

Larry Malone was an older man, at least in his sixties, also listed as a senior scientist. And Howard Wise was another molecular scientist. While he had a LinkedIn profile, no picture was attached, and he didn't seem to use the account at all.

I saved images of all the victims then looked at the video footage Marina had sent.

This time, I scrolled back to earlier in the day, around six thirty. Ed had told me he'd arrived at seven and that he was the fifth to get there, so I focused on the camera that covered the restaurant's entrance and watched the diners who walked inside.

Courtney and her husband, Aiden, were the first two I spotted. Courtney wore a patterned blue haltered maxi dress with a sinched waist that flowed down over a cute pair of white sandals. It was casual but still somehow had an air of professionalism. On her arm hung a large woven tote bag, and the triangle on the side told me it was Prada. I instantly knew Courtney wasn't the kind of woman who would carry a fake designer bag.

Aiden, her husband, wore a flashy Hawaiian shirt over a plain white T-shirt and a pair of cargo shorts. On his feet were a pair of Birkenstocks. He was around her age and carried himself with an overdone swagger that reminded me of the type of guy who thought he was walking into a WWE event whenever he moved.

The server led them to the table, and sure enough, they moved out of the frame on the left side of camera six, as Dorothy and Rosie had thought.

I took notes as I headed back to the entrance camera.

A few minutes later, Russel and Amir appeared. They were both dressed in nice polo shirts and shorts, with slip-on sandals. Amir was about the same height as Russel, and while I couldn't hear what he was saying, he seemed to be casually chatting with the hostess before he and Russel entered.

Ed arrived next, then Howard and Julia. They walked hand in hand, an older couple. Julia seemed very excited to be there, and finally Larry and Lara arrived. It was immediately obvious they were married, they way they held hands. Lara was almost as tall as Larry, with her black hair in a fashionable bob.

I saved images of the others in screengrabs but had nothing else to do.

And of course, there was always the other side of this. The attack could have been random. Was it simply bad luck that this group was here? I had to investigate that possibility as well.

Yawning, I glanced at the clock on the oven. It was now just after two in the morning. I had to get some sleep. I was sure, given everything that happened, Zoe wouldn't be back home anytime soon.

I headed straight to bed and fell asleep thinking about the case.

Chapter 6

By the time I woke up the next morning, sunlight shone through the blinds, and I squinted as everything from the previous night came flooding back to me. I got out of bed, stumbled to the kitchen to make a pot of coffee, and poured myself a mug, which I took with me as Coco and I went outside so she could do her business.

When I came back in, I found my phone had some messages from Dot.

I was up half the night looking at footage. Still can't find anything firm. What have you all got?

I have the names of everyone who was at the table, I replied. *And photos.*

I sent them along and then added, *I'm going to go back to the hospital this morning and see if I can talk to anyone else. It might be pointless. I spoke to Ed last night. He doesn't think it could have anything to do with his job. I'm not so sure. I'm no scientist, but making a molecule that can potentially teach the body to cure cancer and all our other ailments sounds like a pretty major breakthrough. The kind of thing other companies in the space might want to kill over.*

I agree, Rosie typed. *Is that what the company was doing?*

Yeah, they were celebrating that they finally found the molecule they were after, or built it, or something. I don't know how science works. I'd ask Zoe, but obviously she's been at the hospital since last night.

A corporate move wouldn't be out of the question, but it feels unlikely. Particularly here on Maui. We'll have to see where the evidence takes us.

Okay. I'm going to go to the hospital. I also want to talk to Jake and see if he'll tell me anything about the bomb itself. The sooner we can narrow down a motive for this, the sooner we can decide where to focus our attention.

That sounds good. I'll head over to Dot's place and see if we can find anything else on those videos. Two sets of eyes are better than one, Rosie replied.

Cool. I'll update you soon.

I locked the phone and slipped it into my back pocket, gave Coco breakfast and a chewy bone to entertain her for a few hours, and then headed out.

On the way, I stopped at the Kihei Pie Company, where a few months ago I'd received a year's worth of free pie at a surfing competition, a transfer from Vesper as a thank you for keeping her out of jail for a crime she didn't commit. I immediately ordered a lilikoi, a chocolate cream, and a banana cream. When I told the woman working the counter that I was taking them straight to the hospital for the staff that had worked the night, she insisted on adding an extra two pies to the order.

That was the kind of place Maui was. We took care of each other, here.

The emergency room was significantly less chaotic this morning. Last night, every spare chair had been taken, and now, only a handful were occupied. If you were going to have a medical emergency, it was usually best to have it before ten in the morning.

I took the pies to the nurses' reception, where Cora still manned the station, but this time, she was speaking with two women. One was tall, with caramel ombre hair that flowed down her back. She wore white ballet flats and a matching pair of pants, a black belt around the waist, and an emerald green silk short-sleeved blouse. On her arm was a brown leather Prada bag, and the way she carried herself screamed confidence. She had to be an executive or something.

The woman next to her looked around the room, her eyes filled with curiosity. Her auburn hair was tied back in a practical ponytail, and she wore a pair of cute sandals with rust-red shorts and a tucked-in black T-shirt with a printed white heart pattern all over it. When her eyes met mine, she offered me a kind smile, which I returned.

I could overhear the first woman as she talked

with Cora. She had a British accent and spoke in a manner that was polite but firm.

"I completely understand your hospital regulations, and I respect that you've got a difficult job to do, but I really do need to speak with the employees. If you'd like, I can give you the direct line for the president of Valantir Technology, and he can confirm my employment in this matter. As a nurse, you understand how critical gathering information quickly is in a matter like this."

Cora shot the woman a sympathetic look but shook her head. "I'm sorry. Right now, there's nothing I can do."

As Cora and the woman continued to speak, the other woman motioned to the pies I was carrying.

"Those look heavy. Can I help you with them?" she asked.

"Thanks, but I'm good. I just need to drop them off with Cora here. Are the two of you working the bombing last night?"

The woman nodded. "Yes. We were hired by Valantir, the company the victims of the bombing worked for. We just arrived this morning from San Francisco. Are you linked to this as well?"

"Hired by the resort to look into it."

"I'm Poppy. Poppy Perkins. And my partner is Ophelia. She's the brains of our whole operation. Listen, why don't we work together? We could use a partner on the ground here who knows the island. And three heads are better than one."

I gave Poppy an appraising look. Normally, I wouldn't accept this sort of help. I wasn't exactly a lone wolf, as much as I liked to think of myself that way, but I had a tightly knit pack that I protected fiercely, and I didn't always take well to outsiders.

But there was something about this woman that I liked. I couldn't quite put my finger on it. She didn't ooze charm and confidence like the woman next to her, but she was solid. Stable. I instinctively trusted her, and I wasn't sure why.

Either working with her would help me solve the case, or she was a serial killer and I was going to end up chopped into little bits and left in the ocean as shark food.

"Let's do it," I replied. "I'm Charlie."

"It's nice to meet you, Charlie," Poppy replied with a smile. Then, she turned to the other woman. "Hey, Ophelia. We're going to let Charlie here take the lead. We're working with her now."

I had half expected that the woman trying to convince Cora to let her in would argue with Poppy. She didn't seem to be someone who took commands well, but at Poppy's words, she paused and turned.

I stepped forward, and an exhausted-looking Cora took a big sip from the jumbo coffee mug at her desk.

"These are for you and your team," I said.

When she put the mug down and spotted the pies, her face broke into an expression of gratitude.

"Oh, you are the best," Cora said. "Thank you so much."

"You've obviously had a night. You all deserve it."

"We have. It's been awful, Charlie. We're up to five dead. One of the people from San Francisco had a heart attack when she found out her husband didn't make it. More injured."

"Is there anyone we can speak to this morning? I'm working with these two women from the mainland."

"Oh, why didn't you say so?" Cora asked, shaking her head. "If you know who they are, then that's fine. You can speak with Courtney Silva. She woke up a few hours ago. She was very upset, obviously. Wanted to speak to the police immediately in case she could help. I asked her if she was willing to talk to you, and her reply was, 'absolutely.' I'll take you to her now."

The three of us followed Cora down the hall through the emergency room to a private room.

"I'm Charlie," I told the British woman quietly.

"Ophelia Ellis. It's nice to meet you."

"Just so you know, if you're secretly journalists trying to get information, I will ruin your life, set the remains of it on fire, bake the ashes into banana bread, and feed it to everyone you love."

"Understood," Ophelia replied, the corner of her mouth turning upwards into an amused smile.

I had to admit, I was impressed. Most people,

facing a threat like that, would have reacted with at least a little bit of shock and surprise. That Ophelia took it in stride told me maybe she wasn't really a reporter.

She didn't give off reporter vibes either.

Cora led us into a private room, and lying on the bed in the center was Courtney Silva, looking much worse for wear than she did in her corporate headshot. She was propped up with pillows, and a bandage covered most of her right temple. A chunk of her hair had been shaved off to do it. An IV was connected to the inside of her elbow, and her skin was pale. Still, even in that state, she looked at me with clear, intelligent eyes that followed us into the room.

"Courtney," said Cora, "this is Charlie, the private investigator hired by the resort to find the person who planted the bomb. And two women who have been hired by Valantir. Are you still willing to speak with them?"

"Yes. Thank you for bringing them in. And thank you for coming," she said to us.

"Of course. How are you feeling this morning?" I asked as Cora gave us all a final glance and left the room.

"I'm fine. What do you need to know? How can I help?"

"Can you tell me about last night? You and Aiden were the first to arrive, weren't you?" I asked, taking the lead on the interview.

I couldn't help but notice the impressed looks that crossed the faces of the other two. I figured they hadn't expected me to do my homework.

"Yes. Do you know how he's doing? Everyone is dancing around the question when I ask. Is he all right?"

"Sorry, I don't have a clue. I'm genuinely telling you the truth. I'm not a doctor, so I'm not privy to that sort of information."

Courtney's face fell, and her shoulders slumped slightly. "Okay. If you hear, can you let me know? I want to be sure he's going to be okay."

"I will," I promised.

"Anyway, Aiden and I arrived first. I'm an early bird—always have been. In my opinion, arriving at an appointment on time is showing the other people at that event that you respect them. I'm the head of the team, and as such, it's my role to arrive first. We were nearly late, because Aiden couldn't decide which shorts he wanted to wear, but we arrived five minutes before our reservation, and I chose to sit at the middle of the table. I wanted to be accessible to my team. We're celebrating." Courtney's voice shrank to barely louder than a whisper. "We were celebrating."

"I've been given bare details about what your company was celebrating," I said. "The discovery of a new molecule that could change medicine as we know it."

Courtney's eyes moved from mine to the other

two, then she glanced down, deciding what to tell us. "That's right. Although you're not supposed to know even that much. It's all extremely secretive. We're not done yet. We need to go through rigorous rounds of testing. We need to get a patent. We need to get FDA approval. It will be years, likely even a decade, even with expedited approvals, before anything we've done sees the market. But we've finished step one, and it's going to be worth billions upon billions of dollars."

"Therefore, there is a strong possibility that one of your competitors might be behind the attack," Ophelia said, voicing my own thoughts.

Courtney paused, her mouth turning into a small *O* for a couple of seconds before she recovered. "I hadn't considered that. It's obscene. Inhumane. But the biotech space is so competitive. I don't doubt that statistically, there are at least a few psychopaths among my competition. But could they do this? It's inconceivable."

"I think you realize it's not outside the realm of possibility, though," I said gently.

"No," Courtney replied slowly. "Although I can't imagine who would be behind this. It would mean that whatever company's employee did this knew about our trip and why we took it. Corporate espionage is a regular thing in our world, but we were very careful. Our team is small. Everyone was vetted multiple times. I'm constantly on the lookout for anything that appears suspicious. Don't you think it could be something else? Maybe one of the groups who wants fewer tourists in Hawaii?"

"I'm considering every option at this time," I replied. "I'll go where the evidence takes me, but I'm not ruling anything out."

"Good. I suppose I don't want to think… if it's someone else in the industry, I probably know them. Have probably spent time with them. I cannot imagine someone whose hand I've shaken, who I've attended conferences with, who I've probably looked in the eye, doing this to my team. I need to get out of here. I need to take care of them. Are you sure you can't tell me anything?"

"I spoke to Ed last night," I told her. "He was in the waiting room. He had a cut on his side but seemed fine otherwise."

Courtney breathed a sigh of relief. "That's something, at least."

"Can you tell us everything you remember in the minute or so leading up to the explosion? What were you doing? Where were you all located?" Ophelia asked.

Courtney closed her eyes, leaning back in her bed. "It's a bit of a blur, so forgive me as I take a second. Let me think. Howard wanted to show me something on his phone, so I'd moved over a seat to have a look, since we had an empty one between us. His wife, Julia, was sitting across from him, but she had gone to the bathroom with Lara. Ed was sitting next to her then Russel. And Amir was next to him.

Aiden was originally sitting next to me in the empty seat, but he moved to sit next to Amir. The two liked to talk to each other at these things, since neither one of them worked for the company."

"What did you think of Amir?" I asked. "I assume you didn't know him well?"

Courtney smiled. "He's a nice young man. Very polite. Friends with Russell. I only met him for the first time on this trip. He and Russell were college roommates. My understanding is that Amir went into mathematics when Russel specialized in biology. Howard was at his seat, next to me since I'd moved over to see his phone, and Julia had gone to the bathroom. There was a server too. She was taking a drink order from Aiden."

I jotted everything Courtney said down in a notebook.

"We were just… living. Enjoying life. Celebrating a good time. What Howard wanted to show me on his phone? It was his daughter; she had sent him a video greeting from her home in Tempe. He was so happy. He wasn't great at using the phone but wanted me to see the video. I don't remember it. That was when it happened. I was just… I wasn't on my feet anymore. I don't remember seeing anything. But there was screaming. My ears were ringing. I couldn't open my eyes. And the next thing I knew, I was here, in this hospital bed. It reminded me of Boston. The marathon. I was there; I'd finished about ten minutes before the bomb went off, and I saw it happen. I remember thinking it was the same thing."

"Did you notice anything suspicious? Anyone who seemed like they didn't belong?"

"No. Nothing like that. And I would have. Believe me, ever since the bombing at the marathon, I've been extra cautious. People in San Francisco told me I was crazy. I really thought this was something random. We were facing the beach. Someone could have simply thrown something onto the patio from there, couldn't they? Were there security cameras?"

"There were, but they didn't cover the table you were at," I replied. "Whether that was bad luck or someone planned it that way, I don't know yet."

Courtney bit her lip. "I'm not a big fan of coincidences."

"No, neither am I."

"What about anything that happened that wasn't suspicious? Does your whole team get along?" Poppy asked.

Courtney smiled, her face beginning to glow as it reached her eyes. "My team is great. We've been working together for four years now, and while I won't pretend that there aren't issues that sprout up, we're a good team overall, and none of the minor issues are anything that would lead to something like this. They're small arguments over how long it's acceptable to leave yogurt in the work fridge, and whether or not mugs should be left to dry in the sink or dried with a towel and put away. That sort of thing. Nothing big."

"Is there anything else you can think of that you want us to know going forward with this investigation?" Poppy asked.

"Not at the moment. I'll let you know if I do. I have to get in touch with my boss at Valantir. There's so much that needs to be done now. We'll have to send out press releases, and I need to know my team is okay."

"All right. Here's my card. Call me if you think of anything. I hope you heal up quickly," I said.

"And mine," Ophelia added.

I took Ophelia's, checking quickly to make sure hers didn't mention any affiliation with a newspaper —it only had a phone number in the bottom corner, with her name in the top corner—and placed both cards on the small table next to Courtney's desk, next to a pair of reading glasses, then headed back out into the hall. Poppy, the last one out, closed the door behind her, and the three of us immediately fell into conversation as I motioned toward the vending machine. "I'm thirsty, I'm just going to grab a pop," I said as I walked in that direction, with the other two following me.

"Thank you for including us back there," Ophelia said to me. "We both appreciate it."

"We do," Poppy agreed. "That at the very least saved us some time. And probably stopped us from having to commit a crime to get into the hospital."

"You're welcome. You're private investigators as well? From California?" I slid a couple bills into the machine and listened for the familiar rattle of the Sprite bottle falling.

"Investigative consultants," Ophelia said. "But yes, Valantir is our client. Ultimately, we're looking for the truth. As you said when speaking with Courtney, it's very early in the investigation."

"If you have access to Valantir, are you able to gather details on their competition easily? Who might be most likely to want this group dead? With some names, I can cross-reference them with people flying to the island."

"As can we," Ophelia replied. "And it's a good idea. We will do that."

"What did you think of Courtney?" I asked, slipping my drink into my bag and leading the two women back toward the exit.

"She's responsible," Poppy said immediately. "A go-getter. And a good leader. Did you notice how the first thing she asked was if the others were okay? She cared about her husband, yes, but she also wanted to know how everyone else was doing."

"I agree," Ophelia replied. "And she wants to be perceived as intelligent. The glasses she wore; she doesn't need them."

"How do you know?" I asked.

"I looked through them while you were talking and moved slightly. When I did, the electrical socket on the wall behind her stayed in place. That indicates the lenses have no prescription; it would have appeared to move if I'd been looking through a corrected lens. So, Courtney wears glasses to appear more intelligent, but she doesn't need them."

"Wow, I can't believe you noticed *that*," I said, incredulous. I'd noticed the glasses but had never even considered they might not be real, and I wouldn't have known how to test them without trying them on even if I had.

"Get used to it," Poppy said with a wry smile. "You can't have secrets if you hang out with Ophelia long enough. I'm pretty sure if I ever have kids, she'll know I'm pregnant before I do. Then she asked me, "What did Courtney mean when she suggested the bomb makers might have been a group opposed to tourism? Is that a big thing here?"

"There are a lot of people who believe the tourism industry in Hawaii has become too big to support itself and the population," I explained. "They think limiting or banning tourism entirely would allow us to go back to a simpler way of life and better support the people who live here. In particular, the Hawaiians—by which I mean the *kama'ala*, the traditional keepers of this land—who are the most negatively affected by the state's dependence on tourism."

"I didn't realize that sentiment existed," Poppy said.

"They're not exactly going to advertise it on the tourism sites. But occasionally you'll drive past graffiti urging the banning of Airbnb, or straight-up telling people to go home. It's rare; the government really gets on it when it comes to covering up that stuff, but it's possible Courtney saw it, and that's why her mind went there."

"Do you think it could be someone opposed to the tourism industry who did this?" Ophelia asked.

I shrugged. "Anything is possible, but this would be a massive, massive escalation. Most of the opposition is done internally, via lobbying of the government. I've literally never heard of tourists being attacked, ever, let alone something huge like this. I know we can't rule anything out for certain, but I think following that avenue would end up being a waste of time, frankly. Especially given other information, like the table in question just happening to be outside of the range of the security cameras."

"That stood out to me too," Poppy agreed. "A fancy restaurant like that? Most of the tables would have been covered, and it's strange that one wasn't. It makes me think that it wasn't an accident."

"We should speak to whoever was in charge at the restaurant," Ophelia said to Poppy then turned to me. "Would you be able to help us with that?"

"I can send over the contact information for Marina, the manager of the Maui Diamond," I said. "Can I grab a card?"

"Of course. And could we get one of yours as well? We're after the same person. By keeping in touch and working together, we increase our chances of success," Ophelia said, handing me one of her cards. "Now, if you'll excuse me, we're meeting with our third associate to get settled at our hotel. But please, stay in touch. If you need anything, let us know."

"Same here," I replied. Ophelia held out a hand for me to shake. Poppy offered me a smile, which I returned, and the two women headed toward the exit. I tapped Ophelia's card against my palm as I watched them leave.

Chapter 7

When I reached the front desk, I stopped in front of Cora.

"What happened to her husband?" I asked.

Her face fell and she leaned forward. "He didn't make it. Declared dead at the scene. We're trying not to tell her for as long as possible. She keeps asking, but it's going to upset her, obviously. Right now, she needs to heal, not grieve."

I shook my head. "That's awful."

"It is. Nothing like this has ever happened here. They're saying on the news that they don't know if the bomb was set there by someone trying to ruin the reputation of the island."

I shrugged. "It's possible. You never know. All it takes is one person with a vendetta and an internet connection."

Cora shuddered. "The whole thing is awful to think about. Find who did this. Will you, Charlie?"

"I'll do my best," I replied.

I said goodbye to Cora and headed back out to the parking lot.

When I hopped back into Queenie, I pulled out my phone and dialled Dot.

"You've got us both on speaker," she answered.

"I've just left the hospital. I spoke with Courtney, the head of the team. She doesn't know much, but I've got a seating plan for their group. Also, can you run a name for me? I ran into two women who claim to be investigators working on behalf of Valantir, also trying to solve this case."

"Anything suspicious?" Dot asked.

"No, but I want to be sure. The names are Poppy Perkins and Ophelia Ellis."

"Ophelia Ellis, did you say?" Rosie asked.

"Yeah, why? Have you heard of her?"

"I have, although it was a few years ago, now. She's British. I hadn't realized she'd moved to America."

"She had a British accent," I confirmed. "Who is she?"

"I'm not sure the words exist to properly explain the role she played, but she used to involve herself in international affairs. She was a behind-the-scenes player, not one for the limelight. And while she took jobs, she was known for having her own set of morals and rules that she followed, in a good way. She was hired by a man who ran a blood diamond operation and was involved in the enslavement of local people for profit. He hired her to trick the local government into allowing him to expand his mine beyond what was legally allowed, and when she realized what was going on, she pretended to work for him while gathering a case against him. When she was finished, the Belgian government put out an arrest warrant for the mine's owner, a Belgian national."

"And he was put on trial?" I asked.

"He was. Initially, he evaded arrest and made his way to Indonesia. Then one day, a cargo plane arrived in Brussels, and when they began unloading one of the bags, it started moving around. They unzipped it to find the owner in question, his hands and feet wrapped in duct tape and a gag stuffed in his mouth. He was promptly arrested and tried for more human rights violations than I've got hairs on my head."

"Wait, how do you know this, Rosie?"

"I keep an ear out," she replied cryptically.

I shook my head. There was no one in the world who intimidated me more. Well, maybe Dot. Those two together were a force.

"I'll still run their names and see what I can find. Are you on the way?"

"I am," I confirmed. I said goodbye and ended the call. Then, as I pulled out of the parking lot and onto the street, I decided to go up Main Street and stop for a coffee on the way. As I did so, I spotted my mom's car parked along the side of the street.

That was a bit weird; Mom almost never came up to Kahului if she could help it. She liked to stay in Kihei and walked wherever she could. She normally took the car out once a week to go to Safeway for groceries.

Immediately, I wondered if someone had stolen her car. But no, I spotted her, up ahead, walking into a lawyer's office.

Mom had a lawyer? What did she need a lawyer for?

Still, I beeped the horn a couple of times lightly in hello. Mom turned, spotted me, and looked surprised. Then, she raised her hand in a wave and went inside. Weird. I would have to ask Mom later why she was going to a lawyer's office. Was everything okay with her?

Forty minutes later, I was back at Dot's apartment.

"I confirmed that Ophelia and Poppy are working for Valantir as investigators," Dot said as soon as I walked in.

"Great. In that case, I'll give Marina Ophelia's number," I replied, pulling out my phone and the business card and sending a text. "I hope that, with all of us working on this, someone will solve it quickly. Ophelia is smart. I know that from talking to her. And Poppy."

I caught Dot and Rosie up on everything I'd found out at the hospital, and then Dot gave her own update.

"We tracked down the man Marina said was fired three weeks ago. Derek Wolsey. He's got a new job now. Working at one of the stores that sells snorkel gear to tourists on South Kihei Road. We can go down there now and see if he's working," Dot said.

"Great. You got the details I sent about the people at that table?"

"We did," Rosie confirmed. "It's good to know. There is a lot of chatter online as well."

"I bet," I said. "What's the narrative coming out?"

"Well," Dot said, "this is blowing up online right now. Listen."

She turned to the computer and tapped at the keys for a minute. She opened Spotify and navigated to a podcast called *Tom Kidd Rules the World.*

"Ugh, not this guy," I said, scrunching up my face in a grimace. Tom Kidd was one of the biggest podcasters in the world. He'd signed a deal with a major network for over seventy million dollars two years ago and immediately moved to Maui, where he famously bought a multimillion-dollar, multi-acre home in Lahaina, right next to the ocean and the Plantation Golf Course.

Ever since moving here, he complained about Hawaiian residents. How rude we were. How this island wasn't nearly as good as everyone made it out to be. How we weren't welcoming. Of course, these grievances were on top of all the other complaining he did with his guests.

Every week, Tom Kidd brought someone on to talk about a specific topic, and the topic in question was always some sort of fabricated outrage and always fit the same kind of mould.

Men weren't allowed to be real men anymore, society was going down the toilet now that women could—gasp—have their own bank accounts, the poor were leeching off the hard-earned money of the hard-done-by billionaires who had every right to union bust for their own bottom line, and other such gag-worthy opinions.

Dot scrolled the mouse forward and pressed Play, and the man's voice came through the speakers.

"By now, I'm sure you've all heard about the attack at the Maui Diamond Resort last night. That's right—I'm calling it an attack. And I know the woke media doesn't want me to say things like that, because the police haven't confirmed it's a bomb at the time of recording this—it's just after midnight right now, by the way. I knew my listeners would want my cutting-edge reaction, and as soon as I heard about it I came home. Because here's the thing: I was there. I was one of the patrons at the restaurant when the bomb went off. And here's the thing: your boy, Tom Kidd, was the target of that bomb."

He paused for a few seconds, obviously to let the gravity of the situation set in.

I turned to Dot and raised my eyebrows. She motioned for me to keep listening, while Rosie muttered under her breath, "I wish he had been."

Tom continued. "That's right. This is a very special episode of my podcast. There aren't any guests tonight. No, it's just me in the studio, with Peter, who answered the call and came right over when I told him what I needed to do. This is why Peter is more than just a sound engineer: he's my friend. He understood how important this was and how I needed to get this information to you, my loyal listeners, as quickly as possible."

I rolled my eyes. "I wonder if he's ever going to get to the point."

Tom continued speaking. His voice was slightly nasally, just enough to be annoying. How had the guy ever listened to a recording of his own voice and thought, "You know what? I need to be on a podcast"? No, he had a voice for modeling.

"Now, the police won't tell you this. They want to keep it under wraps. And I respect the police. I really do. They get a bad rap in society when they do a harder job than any of these communist hippies whining about them, because they want that tax money so they can keep smoking weed and drinking oat milk lattes. But here's the thing: the police think they're protecting me by keeping this under wraps.

But I'm Tom Kidd. You all know me. I've never been the sort of guy to hide that I have haters. I have them. All the best people do. I was on the phone with one of my buddies just after this happened. Runs one of the biggest social networks that's ever existed. You all know who it is, but I won't name him for his privacy's sake. Anyway, this guy, he tells me, 'You know what, Tom? When people are out there trying to stop you, that's when you know you're doing something right. People are listening to what you have to say, and they know you're spitting truth people aren't ready to hear. And someone trying to kill you? That's next level, but it means you have to keep going. You're doing good. You have a responsibility.'"

I rolled my eyes. "A responsibility? Seriously? All this guy does is complain about how society doesn't let annoying straight white dudes like him get away with literally anything anymore. He goes on about how people like him are getting cancelled all over the place then signs a deal worth more than most people will ever earn in a lifetime."

"I know listening to him speak is worse than sticking a burning hot fork directly into your eye, but keep listening," Dot said.

"Does he actually make a point, or does he just keep jacking off to the sound of his own voice?" I muttered.

Dot pressed Play again, and I silently apologized to the universe for whatever sins I'd committed in a past life that had condemned me to this particular circle of hell.

"Now, I mean it when I say it should have been me. The bomb was meant for me. Whoever did this, they knew they had to do it that way. I'm a former MMA fighter, I know how to handle myself in a fight. And I'm going to tell you how I know. Let's set the scene for last night: I had a reservation at La Mer. It's incredibly difficult to get into, because it's run by one of these celebrity chefs whose head is so far up his own ass he can taste breakfast. I don't like these places, normally. I'm more of a burgers-and-fries kind of guy. Ribs. Like a real American. But this was a business meeting and an important one, so I had to make concessions. It was me, my accountant, my financial planner, one of my lawyers, and five beautiful women I was going to enjoy later." Tom chuckled in a way I was sure was meant to be suggestive but instead screamed "I'm not allowed within five hundred feet of elementary schools."

My eyes rolled so far into the back of my head I felt like a chameleon.

"Problem was, the restaurant, they hadn't factored in my fame. My assistant made the reservation, and she's gorgeous, with the best tits you've ever seen, but sometimes she forgets things. God gave her big tits but took that mass from her brain, you know what I mean?"

Peter laughed. "Whoa, Tom. You know you're going to get comments from feminazis for that one."

"Hey, I'm just telling it how it is, man. Anyway, my assistant didn't think to book a table that offered a bit more privacy, so we get to the restaurant, and they take us to a table outside on the patio. Gorgeous view of the water. I can't deny that. But within two minutes of sitting down, I'd already been stopped by fans three times along the beach. You know who's the most welcoming to me by far on these islands? Tourists. People from *real* America. Indiana. Ohio. Of course, I obliged. You know me. I'm a man of the people. Tom isn't the kind of guy to say no to a picture with a fan."

Right. Nothing screamed "down-to-earth and totally normal dude" like referring to yourself in third person.

"So," Tom continued, "I asked the waitress if we could move. I love my fans. You all know that. But this was a business dinner, and I had to focus on what was going on. I'm a baller, you know. I have big plans for the future. Big ambition, like any real man should. And trust me, you all want those plans to go forward. But that meant I needed privacy. So, the waitress told me initially it wasn't possible. They were all booked out. I asked for the manager, and he made it happen. We were moved to a private table inside the restaurant, and the group that was supposed to have that one got mine."

"Wait, so let me make sure I've got this

straight," Peter interrupted. "The table that the bomb went off at was supposed to be yours?"

"That's exactly what I'm saying. That bomb was meant for me. Someone wanted me dead, Peter. And I'm sharing this with you to tell everyone I'm not scared. This isn't going to stop me. Just because someone tried to kill me, I'm not going to stop sharing the truth with my fans."

Dot turned off the recording.

"Well, that certainly changes things," I said.

"It does," Rosie agreed. "If Tom Kidd really was the target, it opens up a whole new suspect pool."

"Yeah, anyone with half a brain," I muttered.

This case had just been blown wide open.

Chapter 8

"Okay," I said. "We have to consider that Tom Kidd could have been the real target. If whoever left the bomb had access to the reservation list, they could have snuck underneath the table and left it there earlier in the day somehow. They might not even have known that Tom had moved."

"Yes, I think that's a possibility," Rosie said. "Tom Kidd is one of the most controversial people in the country these days."

"It wouldn't surprise me to find out he's actually committed crimes, either," I muttered. "People like that, they always think they can get away with anything. Maybe someone finally tired of him. But instead, they failed miserably and killed and injured a bunch of scientists."

"Okay. Factoring all of this in, let's go visit with Derek Wolsey for now," Rosie suggested. "We can't do anything about this new information at the moment, but we know Derek had a possible motive for leaving the bomb."

The three of us got up and headed out, hopping into Queenie and driving down South Kihei Drive. Seal the Deal Swimming and Snorkel Gear was located right on the main road, offering tourists a one-stop shop for everything they needed to get out on the water at Kam 1 across the street.

As we entered the store, we saw groups of families waiting for their gear. Along the wall to the right were flippers in every imaginable size, the toe colours different for each size. On the left wall were hundreds of snorkel masks. Between sat benches for people to try on the flippers, and among those benches were displays of other accessories.

Against the far wall were branded rash guards and flip-flops for sale. A half dozen staff members moved confidently around, helping customers. Behind the counter at the front, a huge TV displayed underwater footage of someone floating near a *honu*—a green sea turtle, protected by Hawaiian law. It was illegal to get within ten feet of the creatures, and the videographer was keeping his distance but still managed to get the turtle's expression in frame as he floated lazily along, letting the current drag him through the water.

I let Dot and Rosie take the lead on this, since they'd done the research and knew who we were looking for. We waited around for a bit, with me checking out some people. When a family cleared out, armed with snorkelling gear, Dot walked up to the man who had been serving them.

"Derek Wolsey," she said, and he looked slightly taken aback.

"Yeah? That's me." Derek was in his twenties, with a shock of curly red hair that sat on top of his head and made him look like a shoo-in to play Beaker in a live-action version of *The Muppet Show*.

"You know why we're here, don't you?" Dot asked.

"Do you need snorkel gear?"

"Don't play dumb with us, young man," Rosie said. "You worked at the Maui Diamond resort until you were fired three weeks ago."

"Yeah, and it was bullshit," Derek replied, his brow furrowing. "But I didn't set off that bomb. Seriously? You think I would do something like that?"

"You tell us. If it was such bullshit you were fired, maybe you decided you wanted to get some revenge on the resort."

"No way." Derek shook his head. "No. I had nothing to do with that. Was I pissed I got fired? Yeah, of course I was. But it's fine. I have another job now. I got one almost immediately. I moved on from that place. Besides, I'm happier here."

"Tell us about the job. We saw the report from the resort that you yelled at a customer, but we want to hear your side," I said, sympathetically. "Help us understand both sides of what happened."

"Sure, I can do that." Derek looked around the store. "Come with me. Outside. I don't want to talk about it here."

We left the building and stood in the parking lot. It was getting hot; the sun beat down on the pavement, and we walked around the corner, where the building's shade offered a respite from the heat.

Derek ran a hand through his hair. "I know what the resort said, and it was a lie, okay?"

"You didn't yell at that lady?" Dot asked, raising an eyebrow.

"No. I mean, yeah, I did, okay? But it's not like how they said. She was the worst person. Do you know what it's like, working at a place like that? Maui Diamond Resort brings out the richest of the rich. People who make in a day what I make in a year. And they let you know it too. They treat you like garbage. Like the entire meaning of your existence is to do what they want, regardless of anything else."

I nodded. "I know the type."

"It's wild. So, this lady—I was working the concierge desk, right? And she comes up, and she's looking for a table at La Mer. For that night. I tell her, obviously, we're all booked out. We book out basically within five minutes of opening the portal, every single day. After that, there are cancellations. That's the only way to get a table there. I told her that."

"And let me guess. She didn't think that was acceptable?" I said dryly.

"She accused me of lying. Said that she knew we kept tables aside in case celebrities come by. That she wanted one of those."

"Is it true?" Dot asked.

Derek shook his head. "No. I know some restaurants do that but not Maui Diamond. We had Beyoncé call to get a table last year, and we had to turn her away. Mind you, *her* assistant was very nice about it. Anyway, so this lady wouldn't believe me when I told her there were no more tables. I offered to put her name on the cancellation list, but that wasn't enough."

"So what happened? Surely you've dealt with unruly customers before," Dot said.

"I have, but she was next-level. After I made her that offer and she refused it, she asked if I knew who she was? Then she said if we were in Cincinnati no one would dare refuse her a table."

I snorted. "If we were in Cincinnati right now, we'd be under two feet of snow."

Derek cracked a small smile. "Right? She started losing it, and then her husband comes over, and she tells him that 'this little C-word'—she said the actual word—didn't understand how important they were and that I wasn't getting them a reservation."

"What happened then?"

"The husband threatened me, and I said I was going to have to call security. I picked up the phone, and she hung it up and said some stuff I'm not comfortable repeating. About my mother. And that's when I lost it on her. My mom died two weeks ago."

"Oh, I'm sorry," I said, my eyes widening.

Derek swallowed hard, blinking quickly. "Thanks. Cancer's a bitch. And when she said that, I just lost it. I couldn't handle it anymore. So yeah, I screamed at her. I honestly don't even remember everything I said. It wasn't nice. But she deserved every word. Security came, they were taken away from me, my manager was called, and I was taken into his office. He came in a while later. Told me I was fired. I didn't even argue. I'd had it."

"Did you tell him what she'd said about your mother?"

"No," Derek said, shaking his head. "I don't know if it would have made a difference. If I hadn't been fired, I was going to quit anyway. I'd had it. I was so sick of those people. I was sick of being treated like a steaming turd on the sidewalk every minute of every day. Like I was a more useless version of the Alexa that sits in their homes."

"How long until you got the job here?" Dot asked.

"The next day. A friend of mine works here and told me they were hiring. She put in a good word for me. And it's better. The people who come in here are normal, for the most part. Sure, it's not all roses all the time. That's customer service. But it beats being treated like dirt just for existing every single day."

"You don't hold any grudge against the resort?" I asked.

"No. I didn't like the job, but fuck, setting off a bomb? Never. I'm not a psycho. I wouldn't do something like that, no matter how much I hated them. Besides, I heard it was just random tourists that got hurt. If I'd done it, don't you think I would have gone after management somehow?"

"Do you have access to the seating list at La Mer?" Dot asked.

"Nope. I could have looked at it when I worked there, but I was locked out of the system when I was fired."

"What about the security cameras?" Rosie asked. "Did you ever see them? Did you have access? What employees would have been able to?"

Derek shook his head. "No. Management had access, obviously. And anyone who worked in security. But the rest of us, no. There was no reason for us to. Security was in a special office, and none of us had a key that would open that room."

"Did you know what parts of the restaurant were covered by the security cameras?"

"No. I know it wasn't all of it. They liked to keep a few tables outside of the view of security cameras. They put the most important people at those tables. But I don't know which ones they were.

And that might not even be true. It's the rumour that was going around among employees, though."

I nodded. That actually did make sense. A place like La Mer attracted a lot of celebrity clientele who would require privacy. And, as much as I hated to admit it, that matched with what Tom Kidd had said. He would be considered one of those high-profile VIPs who would be given a table outside of the views of the security cameras.

"Where were you yesterday?" I asked. "All day, not just at night."

Derek shrugged. "Here in the morning. My shift started at seven thirty, half an hour before we opened. I was here until five, and then I went straight to a bar to meet a buddy to catch the rest of the Giants game. I got there around ten past five. Here's his number."

After pulling out my own phone, I typed the number into a new message bar and composed a quick text.

Hi, I need to know at what time Derek arrived at the bar to watch the game last night.

"And here's a picture I took," Derek continued, swiping up to get out of his contacts and opening his photos. He showed me a selfie of him at the bar, with Oracle Park in the background, time-stamped at five seventeen.

My phone binged, and I got a reply.

Who's this?

Someone investigating the bomb going off at Derek's former place of work.

Oh. He got there a little after five? The second inning just ended, whatever time that was.

Great, thanks.

"Okay, your story checks out. Can we get the bar's name just in case, though?"

"Sure, we were at Diamond's, just up the street a bit."

"Okay, thank you."

"Can you think of anyone else among your former co-workers who held a grudge against the resort? Or who might have really, truly hated Tom Kidd?" Rosie asked.

Derek smirked. "You're joking, right?"

"Dead serious."

"I mean, most of us hated the dude. Some of the younger guys, who don't really understand how things work, they liked him. Thought he was some sort of alpha, because he's always bragging about how many women he gets with. And the older guys too. They love that he 'tells it like it is,'" Derek said, forming air quotes and rolling his eyes. "But most of us recognize him for the idiot that he is. A dinosaur. A dude who's mad that you can't just stomp all over women and minorities anymore and that saying offensive shit actually gets you in trouble. Theoretically, I guess. He has a lot more money than I do. Maybe I'm in the wrong business. Maybe he's got it right after all. But no, most people there didn't like him. Plus, he's constantly slagging off the island. If you hate it so much, dude, you can always move."

I nodded. "Anyone hate him enough to do something about it?"

Derek's eyes widened. "Like, as in a bomb? Jesus, no. Definitely not. Like, we'd complain about him, but no one I know would actually do something like that. No way. No one I worked with."

"All right, thank you," Dot said. "Feel free to go back to work."

Derek nodded then walked past us back to the entrance.

"We need to talk to Tom Kidd, don't we?" I grumbled as the three of us headed back to Queenie.

"I believe we do," Dot agreed. "Or at the very least, you'll have to. It should be pretty easy to get an interview with him. He's one of those men who loves the sound of his own voice, and the only thing he likes more is ogling pretty women and making them uncomfortable."

"I gathered that much," I said dryly.

Just as we reached Queenie, however, I spotted a familiar car pulling into the lot. It was Liam and Jake, in Jake's new Dodge Charger.

Chapter 9

As Jake emerged from the driver's side, he raised an eyebrow in my direction, but Liam was less subtle. Waddling out of the car, today he was wearing a giant cowboy hat, which I was sure he thought made him look like Indiana Jones.

He looked more like Jabba the Hutt just returned from a vacation in Texas.

"What are you doing here?" he snarled at us. Well, more specifically, at me.

"That hat cutting off circulation to your brain?" I shot back. "Actually, never mind. I don't think that's ever been a problem for you."

Liam scowled at me. "That's harassing an officer of the law."

"Making me look at you wearing that hat is harassing a resident of this island," I shot back. "You look like someone in the early stages of trying to put on a condom."

Dot let out a snort next to me, while Jake shot me a look that said, "Really?"

"Okay, okay, that's enough," he interjected before Liam could reply. "We're all on the same side, here. Charlie, I assume you're working this? Marina told me last night she called you."

I nodded. "You got it. We just spoke to Derek here for, I assume, the same reason you're about to. No point; I don't think he did it. He has an alibi. His friend backed it up. You can talk to the people at Diamond Sports and ask his coworkers to confirm here was here all day, but I don't get the impression he's the killer."

Jake looked at me carefully. "Okay, thanks."

"Seriously? You're going to just take her word for it?" Liam complained.

"Someone set off a bomb at a restaurant," Jake replied. "Right now, the priority is finding out who did it, and that means saving as much time as possible. If Charlie says she looked into this, then I believe her."

My heart swelled with an emotion I wasn't really used to feeling before. Pride? That Jake had listened to me and taken on what I'd found out as a fact. That he was treating me as an investigator, not as someone who was just playing detective as a hobby. That he was defending me in front of his partner, another cop.

Was Jake finally ready to treat me like an equal?

Liam shrugged. "Your call. But if we mess this

up and get called in front of the captain, I'm going to tell him you listened to your girlfriend instead of doing an interview yourself."

"I can handle that," Jake replied.

"Have you heard Tom Kidd's podcast?" I asked.

"Yes," Jake said. "We're speaking to him next. We've organized a meeting with him in an hour."

"Let me come," I implored. "I can help. Believe me."

Jake shook his head. "Sorry. That would be a massive breach of regulations."

"This is important. You know what just happened, and so do I. Let's work together for once. We both know we're going after whoever set this off. We can get there faster this way."

I resisted the urge to point out that the last time we'd both looked for a killer, I had gotten there faster than Jake had.

He looked at me carefully, considering my words, and for a second, I thought he was going to agree. Then, he shook his head.

"No, sorry. I can't. You're right. This case is important. That's why I have to do everything by the book. The last thing we need is for this case to go to trial and for a hotshot lawyer to get evidence kicked out because I let a private investigator I have a personal relationship with investigate the case with us."

"Seriously? What if you never get to trial

because you can't find the bomber, because we're not working together?" I replied.

"We can work together. We can discuss this case, informally, outside of a work setting. But I can't bring you on an official police interview, even with someone who's not a suspect. Sorry, Charlie."

I pouted, and I wanted to retort, but deep down, I knew Jake was right.

"Fine," I finally snapped. "Go do your interview, and I'll talk to him some other way."

"I'll message you later," Jake replied. "I think we can work together. We just can't do it in a way that's going to get any real evidence kicked out of court. I have to think about the long game. It's not enough to know who did it. We have to be able to get a conviction too."

I nodded then headed to Queenie, still a bit stung. I knew Jake was right. Ultimately, it made perfect sense. But I still wanted to go with him to interview Kidd. Doing that would have made everything so much easier.

We hopped into Queenie, and Rosie shot me a sympathetic look. "He's right, you know," she said softly.

"I do, but that doesn't mean I can't be irrationally annoyed at it," I grumbled in reply.

"Irrational annoyance is the best kind," Dot said. "Now, why don't you drop us off at home? Rosie and I can make sure you get that interview with Kidd, and we can look into his life a bit more."

"Right. I'll go back to the resort and talk to Marina. I want to know exactly who knew Tom Kidd was supposed to be sitting at that table and if any of them had anything against him."

"Good plan," Dot said. "If we split up, we can cover more ground in terms of information gathering. In a case like this, that's important."

I dropped the two of them off at Dot's place then drove back to the Maui Diamond resort. As I turned off Wailea Analui Drive and onto the resort property, I was taken aback by how normal everything looked. Pulling up to the front of the resort, no one would know that less than twenty-four hours earlier, this place was a scene of chaos and death. Gone was the police tape cordoning off the front entrance. Gone were the police cars, or any sort of police presence.

Instead, people milled around as if nothing had happened at all. Tourists ambled past, laughing, all sunglasses and sunburns, in their tropical clothes and cover-ups, ready for a day at the beach. They weren't going to let something like ruined lives stop them from enjoying their vacations, apparently.

I parked Queenie and headed inside. A fancy A-frame placard indicated that La Mer was temporarily closed, and a security guard stood by the entrance, the restaurant's doors shut, to make sure no one tried to get a peek inside.

Such was life on an island whose lifeblood was

tourism. Any sign that something was wrong had to be hidden.

I walked to the front reception desk and introduced myself, saying I had to speak with Marina as soon as possible.

The man at the counter told me to have a seat, and I did, on one of the comfortable leather benches in the lobby.

I studied the people walking past. No one seemed the least bit concerned about what had happened only steps away the night before.

On the one hand, I couldn't blame them. These people came here to get away from their regular lives and enjoy their holidays. But on the other, it felt really strange to know that I was standing here where less than a day ago, disaster had struck and five people had lost their lives.

"Charlie?" a voice asked then.

I looked up to see the man from reception.

"Follow me, please. Marina is willing to see you in her office right now."

"Great, thanks."

I followed the man up a set of stairs to the first floor, where many of the hotel's amenities were located. Conference rooms, the gym, an indoor pool —and through a door marked Staff Only. We headed down the hallway to a large, honey-colored wood door.

The man knocked twice, and a moment later, I

heard Marina call, "Come in." He opened the door for me.

I smiled my thanks and entered.

Marina was at her computer, still wearing the same clothes she had been in last night. In front of her sat a cup of coffee I assumed had been refilled a dozen times. There were bags under her eyes, and as she looked at me, she blinked a bit more than usual. I knew a woman who'd been up all night when I saw one.

"What have you got, Charlie?" she asked, and I decided to get right into it.

"Tom Kidd. He was supposed to be at that table last night."

Marina sighed. "I heard him talking about it on his show."

"So it's true?"

"Yes. I checked with Janice, the manager at La Mer, who makes up the seating plans every morning. She had put Kidd and his crew at that table and moved a few of the trees around to hide him from the view of the public walking past. Apparently, he moved the table slightly so that people could still see him then complained when they did."

I rolled my eyes. "That sounds right. Walk me through the entire process of setting up tables."

"Every afternoon, Janice arrives at three o'clock, for a four o'clock open."

"Okay, this restaurant doesn't do lunch service?"

"No. As soon as she gets to work, Janice starts off by looking at all of the reservations we have for the day. All bookings are done online, which ensures that we're not overbooking. She then has any notes that are called in and left by the concierge. Generally, they're things like 'such and such is having a birthday party' and 'this is a special anniversary dinner for our parents, and we'd like to surprise them with a cake.' Others are requests for a certain view, or extra privacy. This happened with Tom Kidd, and she placed him at a table outside of the range of the cameras, as we do for celebrities, and had the palm trees moved to block him from the view of the public walking past on the other side of the patio."

"But that still wasn't enough," I said.

Marina shrugged. "According to Janice, Tom was practically begging to be recognized so he could complain. He wanted to move to another table. Janice had a look at the schedule, and another group that hadn't arrived yet was scheduled to be seated at a different ten-person table. She swapped the two around and didn't think anything else of it. Of course, there was no way she could have known."

"So to confirm, nobody could have known Tom Kidd was going to sit at that specific table until after three o'clock."

"That's right."

"Tom Kidd said the manager who moved them was male; he said 'he.' And knowing what I do about the guy, he takes the use of gendered pronouns very seriously."

Marina rolled her eyes. "Janice was the manager here yesterday. He probably changed her pronouns to make it sound like a man was the decision-maker."

"Good point. How easy is it to access the patio from the beach side?"

"Relatively simple, honestly. There's a two-foot-high barrier that's then two feet wide and filled with flowers that separates the resort from the Wailea beach path, and that's it."

"You don't normally have problems with it?"

"No. Our guests want the uninterrupted ocean views. The barrier acts as enough of a separator. We've never seen anything like this happen before."

"And who has access to the seating plan once it's been established?" I asked. "Who would have known ahead of time that Tom Kidd was going to be at the restaurant last night?"

"The reservation was made in his name, so anybody who works at La Mer could have gotten into the system and seen it if they knew to search for him."

"And other resort employees?"

"If they were physically in the restaurant and used someone else's login information to see the upcoming reservations, I suppose it's possible."

"Is there any way to see a record of that?" I asked.

"No," Marina replied.

It didn't seem particularly likely to me anyway. What were the odds that someone from outside the restaurant just happened to look at the list of upcoming reservations at La Mer on the off chance that someone they hated enough to try to murder with a bomb would be seated there soon? No, the odds of that were astronomically low.

That left the restaurant staff as most likely to have seen Kidd's name and decide to do something about it.

"Can I talk to Janice?" I asked.

"Sure. She wanted to come to work in case she could help, but I insisted she take the day off. Here's her number."

"Thanks. Have you gotten any sort of threats lately?"

Marina shook her head. "No. We receive the occasional email accusing us of profiteering off the land, or people telling me we're contributing to the slow death of these islands, but it's never been more than emails, or the odd comment left on social media posts. Never anything that I would even consider a threat. I know it's possible this was an attack on the resort to send a message about tourism in Hawaii, but I honestly doubt it."

"Have you got any guests here beyond the group at that table that you know are linked to the phar-maceutical industry?" I asked.

"I can get someone to find out for you."

"Thanks. I'd appreciate that. I think that's everything for now. I'll leave you; you're obviously busy."

Marina nodded. "It's been just an awful eighteen hours. I don't even mean personally. I'll survive. But we lost an employee last night to this senseless attack. I've spoken to Emily's family this morning, and I didn't have the words. No one should be killed just for doing their job. No one."

"I agree. I'm doing my best to find the killer."

"Thank you, Charlie. You know the drill. Anything you need, you've got it from us. I'll be in touch."

I left Marina's office, and as I was heading back out the front door, my phone began to ring. I checked the caller ID; it was Mom.

"Hi, Mom," I said to her when I answered. I grabbed my sunglasses from my bag and slipped them back onto my face as I exited the building. The sun's rays blasted me. It was late February, but the sun still shone hard every day. That was one of the things I loved about Hawaii.

"Hi, Charlie. Was that you I saw earlier this morning, honking at me?"

"Sure was."

"What were you doing up in that part of town?"

"Working. You heard about the bomb that went off at the Maui Diamond? I've been hired by the general manager to get to the bottom of what happened."

"Is Jake working on it as well?"

"Yes."

"You know, men don't like it when their girl-friends take too much of an interest in their work. I know your job is separate, but the two of you are too close that way. You shouldn't be out there hunting killers, Charlie. It's going to ruin your relationship. Get a job that doesn't make him feel emasculated."

"As much as I'm enjoying this moral lesson that sounds like it's come straight out of an episode of *Leave It to Beaver*, I'm going to remind you that like the bomber, I also have a big red button to press, and I can always hang up on you."

"Charlie, you need to think about these things."

"No, *you* need to *stop* thinking about these things. What were you doing going to a lawyer's office? You could have called Zoe's mom."

The other end of the line went silent for about three or four seconds. "Oh, it wasn't a criminal matter, so Julia wouldn't be able to help. Besides, she's half-retired now, so I didn't want to bother her with work. I was, um, updating my will, actually."

"Found a new sibling you never told me about that you have to add in?" I joked.

"No. Nothing like that. I, uh, actually—I was going to add Jake into my will. You know, just in case."

I narrowed my eyes. "Jake? Into your will?"

"Yes. The two of you are getting more serious.

We both know that. And I want him to know that he's welcome into this family. It's not a big thing. I don't plan on dying anytime soon, Charlie. But I'm getting older, and so I have to think about these things, you know?"

"Uh-huh," I replied, thoughts swirling through my head. "But we're not married yet."

"I know that, but I also know how you young people are these days. I saw a clip on the news about it the other day. You're all so much less into it than we are. For your generation, it's more of a contract. I don't understand it, but I'm trying to. Anyway, because of that, I'm just seeing a lawyer. Jake's not getting much. Don't worry. Just a few little things around the house. I just want him to know that he's important to me too."

"Okay," I replied slowly. Something weird was going on here. This was the same mother who once told me that I had to let a man sample the milk before he bought the cow but that the cow should never be given away for free.

"Anyway, it's nothing to worry about. I just thought I'd call and update you."

"Cool, thanks."

I said goodbye to her and ended the call. I was sure of one thing: she was lying to me. Jake wasn't added to the will. Whether she'd been watching the news or not, that went against everything my mom believed about men, and I knew she hadn't changed her mind because of a single segment on *The View* or whatever.

Mom had gone to see a lawyer, and she didn't want me to know why.

Well, I was going to find out.

Chapter 10

First things first, I called Jake, leaving the phone on speaker as I continued driving up the road.

"Hey, Charlie. What's up?"

"Okay, first things first—if you see my mom and she says something weird about you being in her will, don't freak out. She's lying."

"Good to know, I guess?"

"I don't know why she's lying, but I'm going to find out. Secondly, how did your meeting with Tom Kidd go?"

Jake sighed. "Honestly, we didn't get much out of him. He loves to hear himself talk, but he knew nothing that could help us actually get to the bottom of this. It was a dead end."

"Should have let me come."

"No, I shouldn't have. Listen, do you want to grab dinner tonight? Talk this case over? I have some information about what the bomb was made of. I'll text you some of it. I figure we can share info, and even though we're mostly working separately, that might help us both figure this out."

I smiled inwardly once again. Jake was actually agreeing to work with me. Sure, he wanted to keep some distance, in the interest of keeping his case separate from mine if the matter went to trial, but this was a massive improvement on the last time, when Jake suggested we work together and he didn't actually give me anything. He just wanted to know what I'd figured out.

"Sure," I said. "That sounds great."

We organized to meet at MonkeyPod Kitchen, a restaurant in Wailea that had an amazing pesto and Kahlua pork pizza, and I told him goodbye right as I pulled into Dot's apartment complex. After parking the Jeep in a visitor's spot, I went upstairs to find her apartment now doubled as a Forever 21.

There were clothes everywhere. Clothes that were probably from the sixties, when Dot was a fashionable young adult. The whole place smelled like a mothball factory.

"Is there something you're not telling me?" I asked as I walked in, looking around.

"We're trying to decide what you're going to wear to your interview with Tom Kidd," Dot replied without looking away from the computer.

"None of this, unless the dude happens to have

a thing for smelling like the chest in the far end of the attic."

"Oh, it's not that bad," Dot grumbled.

"It is that bad. If I had allergies, I'd be main-lining Benadryl right now."

"Well, we need to get you dressed up somehow."

"I'm almost afraid to ask."

"Dot has created an all-new identity for you," Rosie explained. "You're now Becky Byrd, an up-and-coming podcaster with her own following on Instagram. Your account has fifty thousand follow-ers, and you're looking to interview Tom Kidd about who wants to kill him. I organized the whole thing. You're a twenty-two-year-old woman whose podcast is all about men and dating. You're a naïve young woman just trying to make her way in modern life, and Tom Kidd fell for it perfectly."

I raised my eyebrows. "What if he actually looks into the podcast that doesn't exist?"

Dot grinned. "Oh, it does. Thanks to the beauty of artificial intelligence, it was pretty easy to create a podcast using a voice that more or less sounds like you. I also generated some images of you, and now we just have to dress you like you're about eight years younger. And do your makeup. Then we can go. The meeting is at one."

I glanced at my phone. It was just after eleven. "Okay. Well, I'm going to head home, then, and put on some clothes that won't make it look like I raided my grandmother's closet. Are you two coming?"

"We will but separately. We've got our own plan while you're interviewing him. All you need to do is pretend to be the young ingénue, and he'll tell you anything. I'm sure of it," Rosie said.

"Men like him are extremely predictable," Dot added. "I know it won't be the most fun you've ever had in an interview, but we need to know what he knows. He might have something that could lead us to the killer."

"Yeah. Don't worry. I get it. Okay, so I show up there at one o'clock. Do you want to run me through all of the stuff I need to know as Becky Byrd?"

"I have it right here. You're initially from Indianapolis, but you moved here after high school because you wanted something different for your life. You started a podcast with your best friend, who came with you, but she ended up deciding to move back to the mainland and go to college. You kept up the podcast, bringing on guests and having conversations with other people that kept your audience listening, and now you're one of the best young up-and-comers in the podcasting world."

"Okay, got it."

"Tom Kidd is going to like you because you're young, you're a bit flirty, you giggle a lot, and you're basically there to stroke his ego and find out everything you can about him. And you can't let on that you actually want to set him on fire, because that would ruin everything, and we all know the ultimate goal here is to find out who set that bomb."

"Got it."

"Here's a folder with everything you need for your new identity, some equipment you'll need, and instructions on how to use it," Rosie said, handing me a manila envelope and a shoebox. "You're to be at the property at one o'clock. We'll organize to meet again afterwards. And I would take a small weapon, just in case. Men like Tom Kidd, they're not to be trusted."

I nodded. I wished I hadn't put the Taser back in Liam's desk. "Right. I'll see you soon. I hope we'll find out everything we need. Jake didn't get anything from Tom. Said the guy just liked talking about himself."

"That doesn't surprise me," Dot said. "But I think he'll be more likely to open up to you."

"I hope so," I replied.

I left with the envelope and shoebox and headed back home. Zoe's bedroom door was closed, which meant she'd finally had the opportunity to come home and get some rest. I snuck around my own room, doing my best to keep quiet so Zoe could get some quality sleep in, trying to figure out what a twenty-two-year-old would wear.

I was in my thirties now, and as much as I hated to admit it, I was now at the point in my life that I could no longer pretend I was in my early twenties, going to the club every night and partying like there was no tomorrow. When music ordered me to drop it down low, nowadays that meant taking three to five business days to bring it back up.

I pulled out my phone and checked out some young influencers' accounts before deciding on a pair of oversized white pants, a pink-and-white crop top, and, to finish the look, a flowy, white oversized kimono.

While I wasn't exactly the best makeup artist in the world, I was still manageable, and I caked it on thick and heavy in a way that would ideally stop anybody from asking too many questions about my age. I still didn't look twenty-two, but Tom Kidd was in his mid-forties, and I hoped he wouldn't be able to tell.

I completed the look with a pair of thin-strapped white sandals that I usually saved for special occasions. I probably should have had my nails done, but there was no way I could do them myself without making it look like I let a five-year-old give me a manicure.

Instead, I quickly threw some polish on my toes, let them dry, and hoped that it would be enough to let Tom Kidd believe I was actually an influencer.

I drove to the estate where he lived. I pulled off the highway and onto Plantation Club Drive. The road was in perfect shape, not a single pothole or crack in the pavement to be seen. To the left was the golf course, its perfectly manicured lawns spotted with the white sand of the bunkers and dotted with patches of trees that turned into the forests high above and spread into the cloud-topped mountains.

To the right lay the ocean, a perfect blue. Cook pines dotted the side of the road, giving the space a bit of personality. The spot was truly gorgeous, but the money required to own a property here was obscene.

I found the right address and pulled up to the closed gate, which was electronically secured. Facing the camera at the box next to it, I flashed my cheeriest smile. "Hi, this is Becky Byrd. I have an interview with Tom Kidd at one o'clock."

For a moment, no response came. Then a voice called through the speaker, "Go on ahead. Pull up to the front of the house, someone will meet you."

"Thank you so much," I sang as the black gate in front of me slid open. I pulled Queenie up the short driveway to the entrance. This home was huge; one story, with a sleek beige exterior and medium gray roof tiles.

Emerging from the home was a woman who looked to be in her mid-twenties, dressed like she was just about to head out to her shift at Hooters. I wondered if this was the poor woman who Kidd had thrown under the bus in his podcast, who had supposedly booked the wrong table and then been called an idiot for it.

"Hi, Becky," she said to me with a warm smile that didn't reach her eyes. "I'm Lisa. It's so nice to have you here. Let me take you in to meet Tom. You must be so excited."

"Oh, I am," I gushed, lying through my teeth. "He's such a legend in the podcasting industry. I can't believe someone would do something like this to him."

"Me either. I was so surprised when I heard about it last night."

I followed Lisa into the home, and she took me to a living room bigger than my whole apartment. Cream couches and armchairs were set up in a U shape, toward the far wall. French doors opened onto an outdoor pool and perfectly manicured lawn, with a view of the ocean beyond. A large mahogany-colored leaf-blade fan above spun lazily, offering a bit of a breeze. In the corner of the room, a black grand piano was topped with an enormous geometric vase filled with a dozen red-and-white roses.

Lisa motioned for me to take a seat, and I did, in one of the armchairs. Reaching into my bag, I pulled out the recording equipment Rosie had left me with, along with instructions on how to use it without looking like a complete and total amateur. I'd memorized the instructions back at home, and now I clipped one of the microphones to my collar.

Lisa left, and a minute later, Tom Kidd entered the room. In his late forties, wearing his trademark knit ski cap to hide his receding hairline and a thick, black beard that was a shade too dark to be natural, he strutted into the room wearing a button-down shirt with the first three buttons undone and a pair of cargo shorts.

"Becky," he said, coming forward with his arms open, like he wanted to take me into a hug.

I forced a smile on my face and grimaced as he hugged me, holding on for about a second too long. I'd been here all of two minutes and I was already grossed out.

When he pulled away, he motioned for me to sit and took a spot on the seat across from me. "It's nice to meet an up-and-coming podcaster like you. As you know, I'm one of the biggest names in the industry. It's what allowed me to buy this place and live the lifestyle I do. I have millions of followers, and I'm sure yours are going to want to know what's going on here. Because as I'm sure you heard, someone tried to kill me."

"I did hear that," I said, passing him over a microphone, which he expertly clipped to his own collar. "You don't mind if I record, do you? I'd like to put clips of what we say on my show."

"I'd be disappointed if you didn't. Of course, it's also about what's not said into the mic." He winked at me.

I forced a smile while trying my best not to gag.

"So, as I'm sure we all know by now, you were supposed to be at that table where the bomb was detonated," I said. "But the real question is this: who set it off?"

"Becky, the thing you have to understand is that I have so many enemies out there. I have millions of fans, yes. Every week, my podcast reaches eight million people. I'm one of the biggest podcasters in the world. Eight million. Can you even understand that? That's basically as if every single person in New York City listened to my podcast every week. And the one I dropped this morning, after the bombing? It's already breaking every record I've ever hit. Fourteen million people have listened to that episode. People love me. But people hate me too. That's what happens when you tell the truth."

"The truth?"

Kidd nodded. "I make a living telling people the things the government doesn't want them to hear. And I'm not talking about the conspiracy theory shit. I don't think there was anything going on with the JFK assassination, or that there are chemicals in airplane vapor trails. I'm talking about real life, the stuff that affects us day-to-day. While the mass media is out here telling our men it's okay to act like women and be completely emasculated, I'm letting them know that it's still okay to be a *real* man. That you can still listen to Kid Rock and shoot empty beer cans for fun."

"I didn't realize those were things you weren't allowed to do anymore," I said, starting off dryly and then realizing I sounded too skeptical and perking up my voice toward the end of the sentence to hide my complete disdain for the guy.

Luckily, if Kidd realized anything was going on, he didn't let on. Instead, he nodded wisely. "All men are supposed to do these days is paint their nails and be stay-at-home dads. It's ridiculous. It's going to be the downfall of society, and *someone* needed to be out here telling people that it's still okay to be an alpha male, like me. It's okay to like having sex with gorgeous, young women."

If I'd been drinking anything, I would have spat it out at hearing Tom Kidd describe himself as an alpha male.

"So people hate you for telling the truth."

"That's right. So many do. I've been sued dozens of times. I have full-time lawyers on my staff, not because I want to but because I have to. They think they can silence me. The liberals and their ideas. They think they can use the courts to stop me. But it's not going to work."

"Do you have any major lawsuits going right now?" I asked. "Maybe someone involved in that decided they wanted to get revenge outside of court."

"Always. I've always got something going on. Right now, it's a case over in California. Some bitch running for mayor of Los Angeles got mad because I found out she lied on her taxes, and I told people about it. Don't get me wrong—I think our tax dollars are spent badly. But if you're going to come out here and preach about how the government owes people a safety net, and how you want to increase government spending because the lazy homeless want to be supplied with a free house instead of getting their act together and getting a job, well, you better be paying your share too. She wasn't, and she was mad that I showed the voters of Los Angeles—and America, because you know someone like her wants the national stage eventually —who she really was."

"She's suing you for revealing she cheated on her taxes?"

"That's right. She claims that I hacked her computer, that there was no other way for me to get the information, but it's all a load of bull. I have my sources. The old-fashioned kind, because I'm an old-fashioned man. How does she expect someone like me to do that sort of thing? I'm just a normal guy."

Right. A normal guy with a podcast worth millions of dollars. No way was I taking this guy at his word, but I had to pretend.

"You think she could have done this?" I asked.

"Well, I'm not saying that exactly. That would be libel. Or slander. You know, one of the two. I'm never really sure which one applies to spoken word and which one's for written, you know?"

Tom chuckled in a way that was probably meant to be self-deprecating then leaned in toward me, covering up his mic. "Include that part in what you put in your podcast, okay? It makes me sound down-to-earth."

"I will," I promised with a smile.

Satisfied, Tom leaned back in his seat. "I'm not going to say Tiffany Carr is the one who did this. I genuinely don't know. But there are quite a few people out there who don't like me and would do anything to get me off the air. Including setting off a bomb. And here, on the island? Sure."

"I've heard you complain about people on Maui before," I said, taking the opening. "What is it about you that people don't like?"

"My money," Tom replied. "Plus, the fact that I'm a white man. You know, we're actually the most oppressed group of people."

"Are you really?" I replied, this time completely failing to hide the incredulity in my voice.

"It's true. Women love to bitch and complain about being oppressed, but do you know what women don't have to do? The draft. Women don't have to go to war. Ever."

I resisted the urge to reply that it was men who implemented the draft and that he had his own ancestors to thank for that; women had nothing to do with it.

"It's actually much more difficult to be a man than it is a woman," he said. "Especially these days. Everyone is always criticizing."

"Ah yes, a group famous for never dealing with any criticism ever: women," I replied. I would have to get out of here sooner rather than later; I was having more and more trouble hiding the fact that this guy was the human equivalent of a turd sand-wich. So I quickly laughed to make it sound like I was joking then continued. "You were saying the people on this island hate you for being a rich white man?"

"That's right. So many people here, they treat you like you're scum for coming to Hawaii. Coloniz-ing. They say I'm part of the problem, driving up property prices and feeling entitled to come here. Well, guess what, morons? I have a right to live here. Hawaii is part of America. You got conquered a hundred years ago? Get over it."

"Sure. But people don't have to like it."

"They don't. But they're not allowed to try and kill me either."

"Have you gotten any explicit threats recently?"

Tom laughed. "Threats? Lately? I have a whole email address dedicated to that sort of thing."

"Did you hand them over to the police?"

"Look, I love cops. I think they do important work, and I think they get a lot of flack from people who can't take responsibility for their own actions. You want to not have negative interactions with the police? Stop doing crime."

If Kidd continued like this, his face was going to have a negative interaction with my fist.

"I let the police have copies of some of the threats," Kidd continued. "But some of them contain private information I don't want to get out. And I can't trust a lot of people. You have no idea what it's like, not knowing who among the public likes you and who wants to dance on your grave."

"Your life sounds so difficult," I said, trying to sound sympathetic.

"It is what it is. Someone has to stand up to the woke communists in the media and make sure that American can maintain its spot as the best country in the world. Because right now, we're slipping. And I'm going to make sure we don't slide any further. China is out there laughing at us right now. How embarrassing is that?"

"Can I see the threats you didn't show the police? I mean, come on. I'm on your side here," I said, flashing him what I really hoped was a flirty smile. "You know us podcasters. We have to stick together."

Tom chuckled. "Oh, I'm not sure about that. How do I know I can trust you?"

I dropped the tone of my voice, doing my best sultry Demi Moore impression. "Believe me, I'm very good at keeping secrets."

I held Tom's gaze for a few second then bit my lower lip and dropped my gaze to the floor. That got him.

"All right, well, I don't see why you shouldn't be able to. Lisa," he called out. "Get Becky here the pile of threats we didn't show, okay?"

I rolled my eyes; for a so-called alpha male, Tom Kidd sure fell into my extremely-easy-to-spot trap.

A minute later, Lisa rushed in, carrying a box

full of papers, her face white. "I think someone's here, Tom. There's an intruder. The window in the office is broken."

"An intruder?" I asked, my mouth dropping open.

"Call the police. I'm getting out of here," Tom snapped, jumping to his feet. The next thing I knew, he was sprinting down the hall and out of sight.

"Where's he going?" I asked.

"Panic room. He has one in his bedroom, just in case. I have to call the police."

I pulled out my phone and sent a quick text to our group chat. *Someone's here, an intruder.*

If Lisa was right, it meant someone was coming after Tom Kidd again.

And I had a sneaking suspicion it would be whoever set off that bomb. The killer was here, in the house, with me right now.

Chapter 11

"Where's the intruder?" I asked Lisa, grabbing her arm.

"Down the hall, second door on the left, in the library," she replied in a hushed whisper, the terror in her voice obvious. "He came in through the window. I heard him when I was leaving with the box."

I nodded. "Get out of here. Hide somewhere. Or leave if you can. Anywhere, just stay out of sight, okay?"

"What are you going to do?" Lisa whispered, her wide eyes looking at me in fear. "Who *are* you?"

"Just a podcaster getting my story," I lied.

Grabbing the recorder from the table, I shoved it into the pocket of my pants and crept down the hall. I should have grabbed the knife I'd brought in my tote bag, but it was too late.

I didn't need to confront the intruder; I just

needed to see who it was. If I knew who left the bomb, I could find proof of it later.

Despite trying my best to be quiet, every tap of my sandals against the floor sounded like duck feet flopping against the tiles of an outdoor pool. If you've ever heard ducks running around on tile, you know just how loud it can be. The stupid overly large hallway basically acted like an echo chamber.

I grimaced with every step I took, certain that whoever was back there would hear me coming and either make a run for it or try to kill me too. But hey, I was committed to this case.

I burst into the library and found myself face-to-face with Dot.

"You're as subtle as a bear on cocaine that's stumbled into a honey farm," she said.

"Cocaine is an appetite suppressant, or so I've heard."

"I don't think that applies to bears. Haven't you seen the movie?"

"Yeah, and he doesn't eat the people, He just kills them."

"Spoiler alert—I haven't seen it."

"You don't need to worry about spoiler alerts for a movie called *Cocaine Bear*, trust me. It's not *Citizen Kane*. What are you doing here?" I hissed. "The police have been called. They're going to be here soon."

"Don't worry about it. I've got it covered," Dot replied with a wink. "The closest police department is a fifteen-minute drive away, and with the way Tom can't stop whining about this island, I doubt he's going to be on the priority list when the call goes through, even if he is constantly fawning over them like a deranged fan."

"What do you need me to do?"

"You said you have a box of threats out there?"

I nodded.

"Go take pictures of everything you can," she said. "We'll see what we can find. Where did Tom go?"

I grinned. "Ran to his panic room faster than an eight-year-old who's just heard the ice cream truck outside. I don't think he'll be coming out anytime soon."

"Get those photos, then get out of here. We'll take care of this."

I nodded. "Got it."

I headed back out into the main living room. Lisa had left the shoebox full of threats on the coffee table; she was nowhere to be seen. I hoped she'd taken my advice and left.

I pulled out all the letters and began snapping photo after photo. I didn't even bother reading them; I could do that later. Right now, I just needed to get everything I possibly could. I was getting to the end when I heard a man's voice behind me. "What are you doing?"

I spun around and faced a human refrigerator. Six foot six, with a bald head so shiny he could double for the disco ball at the next seventies-themed party he attended, wearing a black polo and pants, the man had a gun out, pressed against his leg. His head moved from side to side, robotically, like a human security camera.

"I'm looking through the threats. Tom wanted me to look at them," I explained.

"There's an intruder. You should leave."

I shrugged. "I haven't seen any sign of that, but okay."

"There's a broken window leading into the office. You need to leave, now."

He stepped in front of me.

I snapped off a couple more photos and shoved the papers back into the shoebox. Picking it up, I got ready to leave, but the man held up his hand, his robotic head still turning from side to side.

"No, leave that here," he ordered.

"This could help me with… my podcast," I said, remembering at the last second that I wasn't supposed to be a private investigator right now. And besides, I didn't know what Dot was doing, but I wanted to give her as much time as possible to get it done.

The human version of a tumbled rock shook his head. "No. Leave it here. Get out, now."

"All right," I muttered, and I got up and slowly followed him. We were near the front door when a knock came.

"Maui Police, open up. We've heard there's been a disturbance."

The man motioned for me to stay back, and I turned the corner and poked my head around while he carefully opened the door.

"Maui Police Department," a familiar voice said. It was Rosie. She was wearing a black wig that made her look about ten years younger and enough makeup so that if you didn't look too closely, you wouldn't realize the person holding the badge was way above the mandated retirement age. She was dressed exactly like Jake did for work, in a navy-blue button-up shirt and beige pants. She looked the man up and down then past him. "I'm Detective Maria Stringer. I received a report of an intruder."

She flashed a badge that looked suspiciously real.

"We don't know where the intruder is. He may still be on the property," the security guard told Rosie.

She nodded curtly. "Where is the owner of the home? Tom Kidd?"

"In a panic room inside his bedroom. It's impossible to access from the outside. Once we've secured the premises, I'll call him to let him know it's safe to leave."

"Good. Is there anyone else in this house?"

"Lisa, his assistant. And a woman he was interviewing. And housekeeping staff. And one other security guard."

"Get them out. Get everyone out, right now. Including you. When I've secured the property, you'll be allowed back in."

"I can help," the man offered, but Rosie shook her head.

"You can, by ensuring that the other innocent people in this home are all secured outside."

The man looked like he wanted to argue, but he acquiesced to Rosie's commanding tone.

I went back and grabbed the shoebox of threats and followed him, shooting Rosie the smallest smile as I walked past. She didn't return it, which was to be expected. She was a consummate professional, through and through.

Lisa was long gone, and I quickly excused myself and left. I knew whatever Rosie and Dot were up to, they could handle it and would be in touch later.

It was getting to be mid-afternoon, which meant traffic on the way back to Kihei would already be bad. I decided to go overland, via the narrow, twisty roads that connected West Maui and Central Maui. Those roads always felt like what the Jeep was meant to drive on, and I had so few opportunities to take them. But the golf course was already well north of Ka'anapali, and I'd rather play on the dusty roads than sit at a standstill in traffic.

Besides, this would give me the opportunity to visit the hospital again and speak with anyone else who was at that table and was in better shape than the day before.

Most of northwestern Maui was outside of the zone that offered cell service, and by the time I dropped back into Kahului, my phone binged a few times, indicating some missed text messages. I parked in the hospital lot to find confirmation from Dot and Rosie that they had both left Tom Kidd's property.

I'd also received a response from Janice, the restaurant's manager. She was at home and offered me her address; I was welcome to stop by whenever.

I messaged her back, letting her know I'd be there in the next couple of hours, then went into the hospital to see if anyone was up to speaking with me.

Amir, Russel's injured friend, had a broken leg on which he'd had surgery. He was a few hours away from being discharged but was happy to talk to me. He was reading a Kindle, which he put down on his lap when I entered the room.

In his late twenties, he had a couple of days' worth of dark stubble around his chin and deep-set brown eyes that twinkled intelligently in the light.

"Another nurse come to look at my cool scar?" he asked with a grin. The way his skin folded easily into the lines on his face told me Amir was a guy who smiled a lot. "Y'all are going to give me a complex when I go back to San Francisco and no one gives me this much attention."

"Sorry, Amir," the nurse leading me to him replied good-naturedly. "This one wants what's in your head. Charlie Gibson; she's a private investigator working for the resort, trying to get to the bottom of it. She wants to know if you're up for a chat."

"To find the person who blew my leg half to bits? Always. It's a preferred topic of conversation in my head right now, so I might as well keep it going with someone who can actually do something about it."

The nurse smiled then turned to me. "He's all yours. By the way, thanks for the pie."

I grabbed a rolling stool from the corner, sat down on it, and rolled toward the edge of Amir's bed.

"Sorry, I'm kind of a bad host right now. I can't exactly offer you a drink," Amir said kindly.

"No problem. I'll settle with information. It sounds like you've thought a lot about what's happened."

"Sure have. They tell me Russel, the friend I came with, didn't make it. It hasn't sunk in, in a way. None of this feels real. It was supposed to be a nice holiday for Russel to celebrate some work thing."

"Did you know what it was?"

"They wouldn't talk about it in front of me. But I'm not an idiot. It was big. I know that."

"You don't work in the pharmaceutical industry?"

Amir shook his head. "No, I'm in computer science. Gaming. I run a small, independent video game design company. But Russel and I were room-mates in college, so I've known him for about a decade."

"Enough that he brought you on this trip as his plus-one."

Amir smiled sadly. "He knew I always wanted to go to Hawaii. I just never had the time for it. He was between girlfriends, and so he told me he wasn't going to be the only loser who didn't bring someone to the island and that I had to take the time off to go with him. He said what they figured out was going to make their company billions upon billions, so the least he could do was make them pay for a few more first-class flights to Maui and comp some meals and drinks. My partner in the business promised he could handle everything for a week, so I went with Russel. Little did I know it was a huge mistake."

"Had you met anyone else you were with before this trip?"

"No, never."

"Did anything stick out to you? What were your impressions of the group?"

Amir raised an eyebrow. "That's pretty vague."

"That's on purpose. You're an outsider. Most of the people there know each other, know the dynamics, have preconceived notions of one another. Not you."

Amir nodded. "Okay, I get that. Yeah. They were a small group. Courtney was in charge, but Larry wanted to be."

"Oh?"

"You could tell, the way he treated her. Larry's older than her by maybe fifteen years. And he was constantly trying to correct her in front of the others. Make her look like an idiot while he seemed like the confident guy with all the answers."

"I know the type," I said dryly.

"And Courtney was getting it from all sides; her husband was the same. Apparently, he works as a manager at a Barnes and Noble, but he wants everyone to think he's a pilot. It would be funny if he was fifteen. It's less funny in his forties."

"I heard about that."

"As for the others? Ed seemed relatively normal, but I think there was something going on between him and Howard's wife, Julia."

"Oh?"

"I mean, it's possible I'm wrong, but I know when two people look a little bit more buddy-buddy than they should. They also both went to the bathroom at the same time, about twenty minutes before the bomb went off."

"You think they were having an affair?" I asked.

"Yeah, I do. Look, I know it's not great. I don't even know if they survived."

"Ed did; I spoke to him in the waiting room."

"All I can tell you is growing up, my sister watched a *lot* of *Grey's Anatomy*. It was literally always on when I was home, and if there's one thing I learned from that show, it's how to tell when someone is cheating. And those two? They were cheating. I would bet money on it."

"Do you think her husband knew about it?"

Amir's brow furrowed. "That part, I'm not sure. If he did, he didn't show it. Wait, do you think he could have done this? Set this off? No way."

"Why do you think that?"

"Well, it would have hurt him, wouldn't it? It couldn't have been anyone at the table. There's no point."

"No, but Julia wasn't there," I said. "Someone else told me she had gone to the bathroom before the bomb went off."

Amir gaped at me. "Shit. You're right. I forgot about that. But… why her?"

I shrugged. "I don't know. If there was a relationship triangle there, who knows? Maybe she was trying to just get rid of her husband. I'm just gathering information right now."

"That's insanely risky, though, isn't it? I don't know a lot about bomb making, but something like that, which would have been set off at the table—she wouldn't have known who she'd have killed or injured."

"As I said, it's just a theory right now. Did you

recognize anyone else at the resort? Not even as if you knew them in person, but did you just recognize their face? Anyone who seemed familiar somehow?"

Amir shook his head slowly. "No, I don't think so."

"Okay, thanks. If you think of anything else, can you let me know?" I handed him a card, and he took it.

"Will do. Not like I have all that much else to do around here. I'm being released today. I think I'll spend a few more days here making sure I'm okay and don't have a medical emergency then fly back home."

I said goodbye to Amir, wished him well, then headed back out into the main part of the hospital. One of the nurses was willing to chat, and I found out from her who all the victims were.

Courtney Silva had survived with injuries, but her husband, Aiden, hadn't made it. Russel McCathy, Amir's friend, had also passed away from his injuries. Howard Wise and his wife, Julia, were both fine, and Larry Malone was dead. His wife Lara had a heart attack at the hospital when she learned her husband died, and she passed away a few hours later as well.

The final victim was Emily Thompson, a server at the restaurant who had been taking drink orders when the bomb went off.

Just as I was about to leave, I spotted Ophelia and Poppy.

"Hey," I said to them. "How's the case coming along?"

"We're making progress," Poppy said. "We've focused so far on the idea that the bomb was meant for the Valantir group. However, we've yet to find any of the competition who are on the island."

I nodded. "Good to know. Are you sure? I have a friend who can compare names to airline seating plans if not."

"Thank you for the offer, but we also have an associate capable of that."

"I also went back to the Maui Diamond and spoke with Marina, the manager. Have you heard about Tom Kidd and his claims that he was the intended victim?"

"The only thing that man enjoys more than hearing the sound of his own voice is the ability to paint himself as a victim," Poppy said dryly.

"My thoughts exactly."

"We have heard his claims. Is there anything to them?" Ophelia asked.

I hoisted a single shoulder upwards slightly. "Who knows? It's true he gets a ton of threats. The police have some. I have the rest. Are they legitimate? That's the question. Also, to hear Marina tell it, for the person to set off the bomb and to have known Tom Kidd was going to sit at that table, a lot of things would have had to come together perfectly."

"Like a plane crash," Ophelia said.

"What do you mean?"

"Have you ever investigated a plane crash?"

"No."

"I have. And they're very, very rarely caused by a single thing going wrong. In nearly every case, multiple issues are at play. In a plane crash, there are almost always at least three or four instances that investigators can point at where if a decision had been made differently, the outcome would have likely been different and the plane would have landed safely. This sounds like one of those."

"It does," I agreed. "I'm going to speak with Janice, the manager, now. I want to confirm a few things with her. But so far, I think for Tom Kidd to have been the intended victim, a lot of things had to happen perfectly. And to use your analogy, while almost every single flight lands safely at its destination, from time to time one plunges into the ocean."

Ophelia nodded. "Yes. I don't think we can entirely discount the idea that Kidd was the intended victim. But I find it unlikely. Our energy is probably better spent elsewhere."

"I wish he was either the victim or the perpetrator here. He's the worst. And meeting him in real life didn't help."

"If only we could say people like that eventually get their comeuppance," Poppy grumbled. "But he got his multi-million-dollar deal and his home in paradise, and he even potentially survived an assassination attempt that instead killed innocent scientists."

"We don't know that for sure yet," Ophelia pointed out.

"I know. But nothing would make me happier than Tom Kidd not making it out of this whole situation with his reputation intact."

"It's good to know we're all on the same page with him," I said with a smile. "If my team happens to come into some information that could help bring him down, do you want in?"

"Absolutely," Poppy replied.

"We have been known to take on cases that are not necessarily within our purview, if we feel the reason is good enough," Ophelia added.

"Great. Good to know you're in if we decide to do this. I'm going to talk to the manager now. Do you want to join me?"

"Yes, thank you," Ophelia replied.

"Great. Do you want a ride? It's no Mustang, but I have the best Jeep on Maui."

"We'll take you up on that," Poppy said with a grin.

The three of us left the hospital and ran directly into Jake.

Chapter 12

"Fancy meeting you here," I said in greeting, looking around for Liam. "Where's Rumpleforeskin?"

"You're a modern-day Shakespeare, truly. He's following up a lead. I'm interviewing a couple of the survivors here at the hospital today. I've just come back from meeting with the explosives expert. Who are your friends?"

"Poppy, Ophelia, this is Detective Jake Llewyn. He's one of the detectives working this case. I've worked with him before; his partner, Liam, is the reason shampoo bottles have instructions, but Jake can be trusted."

A knowing smile crossed Ophelia's face. "Yes, that the two of you are in a relationship tells me you trust him."

"Seriously?" I asked, my mouth dropping open. "How?"

"I told you—secrets are impossible when she's around," Poppy said, shaking her head.

"Are we really that obvious?" Jake asked. "What's your connection to this case?"

"Yes, and we're investigating on behalf of Valantir," Ophelia replied. "Charlie's team and mine have joined forces to gather information and find the person responsible for this attack. What did the explosives expert say?"

Jake's gaze moved from one of us to the other.

"It's fine," I said. "We've checked them out. They're telling the truth. You can trust me."

Jake considered my words for a moment then nodded and leaned casually against the hood of his Charger. I tried not to think about how much I wanted to tear his clothes off right now. Okay, maybe that was why Ophelia had instantly picked up that we were a couple.

"We learned a decent amount," he said. "They confirmed that a burner cell phone was used to set off the bomb. Basically, as soon as someone called the burner cell's number, the fuse was triggered and the bomb was set off."

"Do they know what the bomb was made of?" I asked.

"The bomb maker used peroxide explosives, common ingredients in homemade bombs. This specific one was TATP."

"I've never heard of it."

"It's what the shoe bomber used, or tried to, anyway," Ophelia said.

Jake nodded. "That's right. It was also used in a number of terrorist attacks in Europe in the past twenty years. It's pretty easy to make with ingredients you can find at any pharmacy. It's also highly, highly dangerous. An explosion of even a single gram can cause injury. The bomb didn't have to be big. To give you an idea, TATP is about eighty percent as powerful as TNT."

"How easy is it to make?" Poppy asked.

"Anyone with internet access, nail polish, and hair bleach can get it done, if they're smart enough not to blow themselves up in the process," Jake explained. "And you have to factor in that someone might have gotten lucky. However, the cell phone detonator is a little bit more complex. And there's also the fact that TATP is extremely sensitive. For this to have gone off the way the bomb maker intended, they would have had to be skilled."

"That leads us back to the theory that it could be someone linked to this group, rather than a random person trying to kill Tom Kidd," Ophelia said.

"That's what I'm leaning towards. Of course, we can't be sure. Some people on this island have the skills to make this. Have you found anything else this morning?"

"Just that Tom Kidd is actually a scared little

baby who runs to his panic room at the first sign of intruders."

Jake raised his eyebrows. "That sounds ominous."

"Don't worry, it was just Dot. I also got a bunch of threats that he didn't want to show you for whatever alpha-male reason. I'll send them over later. Let me know if you find out from the survivors anything else about a potential affair between Ed and Julia."

"Will do."

"What have you got?"

Jake pulled out his small notebook and flipped the pages back. "Beyond the composition of the bomb, not a lot. I'm looking into Valantir's competition, and so far, I'm nowhere on that."

"We've done a lot of research on our end. We have a list of their competitors and their employees, but so far, we've got no evidence that any of them are in Hawaii," Ophelia chimed in.

"How do you know that?" Jake asked.

"Oh, we have our ways," she replied with a mischievous smile.

I liked Ophelia. She reminded me a lot of Dot and Rosie.

"It all seems pretty unlikely, though," I pointed out.

"Oh? Why do you say that?" Jake asked.

"The table wasn't supposed to be for that group. It was supposed to be for Tom Kidd, which means that if someone in competition with Valantir was the one who left the bomb, they would have had to do it after the group was already seated."

"Which means someone at that table would have recognized them," Jake finished, nodding in understanding.

"Right. I've spoken to Courtney and Amir now, and neither one of them mentioned anybody they knew being around. Amir wouldn't necessarily recognize a competitor, but Courtney would. And neither of them even mentioned anyone they *didn't* know coming around."

"And we spoke with Howard and Julia Wise this morning," Ophelia said. "Julia is cheating on her husband, although I don't know with who yet. Neither one of them recognized anybody at the restaurant either. We made sure to ask."

"So the alternative is a stranger, but having someone you don't know carry a bomb to a table full of your competitors is very risky," Jake pointed out.

"It is. That's why I don't think that's the track to follow," I said. "The three of us are going to speak to Janice, the manager of the restaurant, now. I'll see you at dinner later?"

"For sure. We hope we'll be a bit closer to an answer by then. Send me those threats Tom gave you, okay?"

"I will."

I gave Jake a quick kiss then headed to the car

with Ophelia and Poppy, strumming my fingers along the edge of the steering wheel as I pulled out into traffic. Ideally, Janice would help us break open this case.

"That was good thinking back there, realizing it would have been almost impossible for a competitor to drop off the bomb without being physically seen," Ophelia said from the passenger seat beside me.

"Thanks."

"I looked into you the other day. I knew your name from the Marion Hennessey case, but apart from that, I can't find much of an online presence," she continued.

"I'm a very private person."

"So am I."

I glanced over at her. "I heard about your involvement in the thing with that slave-trading Belgian miner."

Ophelia turned and gaped at me for a split second, surprise registering across her features.

In the back seat, Poppy laughed. "Wow, you *are* good. I don't think I've ever seen Ophelia speechless before, even for a second."

"How in the world did you find out about *that*?" Ophelia finally asked.

"I've got my sources."

Ophelia shook her head, looking incredulous. "Well, I have to say, you're the first person I've heard mention Antoine Lemaitre in a long time. And officially, I had nothing to do with that case."

"Officially," Poppy said, making air quotes and shooting me a wink as I gave her a backward glance. "You've impressed her, at any rate. It's not often Ophelia Ellis of all people gets knocked off-kilter by someone. Even I don't know about this Belgian thing."

"The important thing is he'll be rotting in a Brussels jail for the rest of his life. And his entire mine was dissolved. No more blood diamonds. No more slavery, at least not at that one location."

"How long did it take you to find him?" I asked, curious.

Ophelia pursed her lips slightly, considering my question. "Seeing as you seem to know the rest of the story—and you must realize, I am massively curious about how, since there were entire teams of government agents who did their best to scour my involvement from the record—I may as well tell you what you don't know. It took a little more than seven months, all in all. I knew he was in Asia, but I lost him in Laos. He swam across the Mekong into Thailand one night, knowing I was onto him, and disappeared from there. But he should have known he couldn't stay away from me forever."

"I'm impressed," I said with a smile. "Although I must say, an investigation like this seems a little bit… I don't know. Low-key, compared to hunting down blood diamond profiteers."

"I go where the work takes me, and I do what I feel is right."

"And if the two are at opposing ends of the spectrum?"

Ophelia shrugged. "I have enough money. I will always do what I consider to be the right thing."

"Why did you leave England?"

"They do make them blunt on this island, don't they? Although you haven't lived here your whole life. You've spent a lot of time in the Pacific Northwest."

"Seriously, how do you know that? That's creepy."

"It is," Poppy agreed.

"Earlier, in the hospital, you mentioned you wanted to get a pop from the vending machine. Regionalisms are one of the best ways to understand a person's origin, and America has so many of them. 'Pop' is a term used primarily in the Pacific Northwest—Washington and Oregon, specifically. On the other hand, someone who had spent their whole life in Hawaii would use the term 'soda,' like they do in California."

I shook my head. "That's insane that you not only know that off the top of your head but noticed it."

"It's my job."

"I did grow up in Hawaii, but I spent about fifteen years living in Seattle. I've been back here for a few years, but I guess not enough for all the habits to have come back. But great avoidance of my own question. Why did you leave England?"

Ophelia's shoulder tilted upward in the slightest shrug. "It was made obvious to me that my presence on the island was no longer welcome and that it would be best if I chose somewhere else to operate for a while."

"You're in exile, then."

"Something like that. I will return, one day, perhaps. The world is like a beach. It appears the same to us, day by day, because we don't realize the undercurrent that's happening, making small changes every time the tide comes in and out. And then suddenly we realize everything has changed, and it's not the way we remember it."

"Do you like America?"

"I do. I like San Francisco. It is a wonderful city."

"And Hawaii?"

"It is a different place. There is no question about it. The spirit of aloha, as I've been told it's called, is visible. People are more relaxed. Appointments are approximates."

"Island time," I said, nodding. "It's a real thing."

"I can see that," Ophelia replied.

"I don't think I could live here permanently," Poppy said. "Although it is a nice place to visit."

"Why not?" I asked her. "Not judging, just curious."

"It's the island time. I know, for the people who

love it, it's great. But I like the energy of a big city. I like feeling as if things are happening. San Francisco is perfect for that. It's perfect for me."

"How long have you lived there?"

"Just a couple of years. I'm actually from Seattle, too. I still say 'pop.' I moved down to San Francisco to get a publishing deal for my book, which I've now got. I do that on the side, while working with Ophelia full-time."

I grinned. "This story isn't going to end up in your next book, right? This isn't some Holmes and Watson situation, is it?"

Poppy laughed. "No, not at all. I write romantic women's fiction. Not a bloody corpse in sight."

At that moment, we pulled up to Janice Imai's home. It was time to see if she could clear up the muddy water that was this case.

Chapter 13

Janice Imai lived in northern Kihei, in an older, small bungalow that was well maintained. The lawn was manicured and surrounded by native bushes and trees. The driveway was unpaved but covered in gravel, with a newer black Honda SUV sitting on it. A basketball hoop and abandoned ball were leaned up against the side of the house.

The three of us climbed out of Queenie and went to the front door, where we were met by a man slightly over six feet tall with broad shoulders, wearing a casual pair of navy-blue shorts and a heather grey T-shirt. His black hair was cut short, and his face was free of facial hair. His large brown eyes were deep set but friendly.

"Hi, I'm looking for Janice. I'm Charlotte Gibson, the private investigator working for the resort. I told her I'd be coming." I introduced Poppy and Ophelia as well.

"Come on in. I'm Kai, her husband. She told me you were going to come by. She's in the shower right now." Kai lowered his voice. "It's where she's been going when she needs to be alone with her thoughts."

"We can come back later if this isn't a good time," I offered, but Kai shook his head.

"No. She wants to speak to you. Come on in. Can I get you anything?"

"I'm good," I said as he led us into a plain but comfortable-looking living room.

Poppy asked for a glass of water, which Kai went to get while we looked around.

The main couch that faced the TV was made of beige cloth. The three of us sat down on it, and when Kai returned with Poppy's water, he took his spot on a stuffed black armchair near a bookcase on the other side of the room. He propped an ankle up on his knee.

"It's terrible what happened," he said. "I feel awful for Emily, but I have to admit, I'm just glad Janice is okay."

"That must have been terrifying for you," Poppy said.

Kai closed his eyes. "You can't imagine. Or maybe you can. I don't know. I've never felt fear like that before. A friend called me and told me there had been an explosion at the resort, and I just… I didn't know what to do. I jumped into my car and drove straight there. Janice sent me a text about two minutes after I heard. She said she was okay. I pulled the car over and started sobbing."

"I don't blame you," I chimed in.

"I had to take the day off work. I had to be there for Janice. My boss understood. There was no way I was getting any decent accounting done today when all I could think about was how close my wife was to this. Do you know who's done it yet? Do you have any idea?"

"We're following a few leads at the moment that look promising. We're hoping to know soon," Ophelia said.

"Looking online, everyone is saying it's either someone who was trying to kill Tom Kidd, or Hawaiian independence proponents trying to kill the tourism industry."

"The latter is possible, but there's no evidence leading in that direction right now," I said.

"I don't believe that's where you'll find the killer," Kai said. "I realize, I'm biased. I don't necessarily believe that Hawaii needs to separate from the United States entirely. I would like to see it, but I don't think it's feasible the way things are run now. Too much time has passed. But I also disagree with the use of violence to reach objectives. Violence will achieve nothing. We need to control the tourism that comes to these islands through legislation."

"Forgive me, but as an outsider I don't know much about this topic," Poppy said. "Hawaii has an over-tourism problem. Is that what you're saying?"

"It does. The government, which is supposed to represent the locals who live here, has been putting the interests of visitors in front of our own people. Tourism only makes up a quarter of our economy. And where does that money go? The majority of it to the bank accounts of the international conglomerates who own the hotels. Into the pockets of the people who buy residential property built for locals and who set them up as Airbnbs, while our beaches fill up with unhoused who can't find a place to live and are moved on by police officers whose priority is making sure the tourists who come here don't see the reality of life it has caused for its residents, in particular for the *kama'aina.*"

I knew Kai wasn't alone in his beliefs. The tourism industry by and large benefited the non-native population of Hawaii, and opinions on how to fix it ranged from bringing in additional taxes on tourism to laws banning short-term rentals to secession from the United States.

However, thanks to tourism bringing money into the state and the international companies who owned the hotels lobbying hard to maintain the status quo, nothing changed much for the residents of the islands.

Before Poppy had a chance to respond, however, Janice entered the living room from the hallway. She rubbed her dark damp hair dry with a towel as she entered, wearing jean shorts and a white T-shirt.

The redness in her eyes betrayed that she had been crying.

"Hi Janice, I'm Charlie," I said softly, standing up and holding out a hand, which she shook.

Kai stood up from his seat. "I'll take your towel," he said, placing a gentle hand on his wife's shoulder. "If you need anything, Janice, just let me know."

"Thanks, babe."

Janice smiled at her husband then came and took the spot he had just vacated, tucking her legs underneath her. "How can I help? Anything you need."

"I mostly want to know the details of what led to that table that night. Marina said you're the one who sets up the seating plan every day?" I asked.

Janice nodded. "That's right. I do. First thing, when I come in, which is an hour before we open. I have to do it that way; it's how we organize the tables to make them fit the size of groups we have every night. I did them myself. I put Tom Kidd's group outside of the view of the cameras. Most of our celebrities appreciate that. Not that I don't trust the security working at the resort, but they don't know that."

"Right. But Tom Kidd had issues all the same?"

Janice rolled her eyes. "Look, I don't want to speak badly of one of our customers, but that was all his own fault. I had the staff move some plants around so that he'd have some privacy and wouldn't be seen by passersby on the public trail. But Tom purposely moved his own chair around so that he would be spotted. He was actively encouraging being seen by the public, and then he complained about it. We swapped his table with another. It wasn't a problem, but come on."

I nodded. "I've met the guy. None of that surprises me."

"No. Some people live to complain. But of course, that poor group. And Emily. I still can't believe she's gone. She was just doing her job. Trying to make money to save up to go to college. And now, just like that, she's dead, because someone set a bomb off in our restaurant. It's unbelievable."

"Did you notice anything suspicious that night? Anyone out of place, who didn't belong? Anyone, suspicious or not, who visited that table who wasn't one of their party?" Ophelia asked.

"I've asked myself the same thing, over and over, ever since it happened. But I can't. I was on the floor the whole time. I would have noticed. This is a very upscale restaurant. And when I say that, I don't just mean the food. I mean every part of the experience. When we're open, I'm always watching, constantly making sure everything is running smoothly. I notice these things. If someone had been there who didn't belong, I would have seen them. But there was nothing."

"Okay, thanks." Something about what Janice said was trying to click with the information I already had, but I couldn't make the facts come together. "What about the group at the table where the bomb went off? Did you meet any of them?"

"Sure. I make a point of introducing myself to as many of the patrons as I can. I met Amir, the young man who accompanied one member of the group. And Larry, and his wife Lara. I also met Edwin, who told me it was their last night on the island. And Captain and Courtney Silva."

"Did any of them seem strange to you?"

"No," Janice replied slowly. "I don't think so. It's hard to know for sure when I only met them briefly, only really for introductions, but nobody stood out as acting strangely in any way."

"If you think of anything else, can you give me a call?" I asked, pulling out a card and handing it to Janice.

"I will. You have to get to the bottom of this. A bomb like this is unlike anything we've ever seen on the island, and tensions are running high. I'm hearing all kinds of rumours. And with Tom Kidd throwing himself in the middle of this and talking out of his ass, he'll only make things worse."

The corners of my mouth curled into a smile. "You're not a fan?"

"Not in the least. He exists only to anger. To rile up a crowd. That's how he gets his followers. He convinces them they have something to be angry about. And a man like that? He's going to take advantage of this. I heard his podcast. He's already blaming us, residents of Hawaii, for trying to kill him. People like him only care about the money, not about what impact their words have on other people."

"I agree completely," Ophelia said.

Janice shook her head. "I just hope you get to the bottom of this quickly, so his fans can put their pitchforks away. I know he has listeners on the island too. He's whipping them up into a frenzy, and I worry that someone is going to do something stupid. This whole thing is awful. Enough people have been hurt and killed already. I don't want it turning into something worse."

As the three of us left Janice's home, I couldn't help but wonder if she was right. Five people had already died. We didn't need Tom Kidd fanning the flames and potentially making things worse. I had to figure out who set off that bomb.

The problem was, none of the puzzle pieces I had lying in front of me seemed to fit.

What was I missing? The answer had to be there somewhere.

We hopped back into Queenie, but before I started the engine, I turned to the others. "I have a couple of friends I'm working with on this case. I don't know what they're up to, but I think we should meet. They're looking into the Tom Kidd side of things, and the more evidence we get, the more I think we should focus on that."

"I agree," Ophelia said. "With Janice's statement, combined with the surviving members of Valantir not having seen anything out of place, I don't believe the bomb was brought to the table by an outsider, which means in all likelihood it was there before the doors opened. Meaning Tom Kidd was most likely the intended target after all."

"And I can believe that, easily," Poppy said. "All right, how about this? We're staying at the Maui Diamond resort. We're in room 401. Why don't we meet there in, say, two hours? We can reconvene and see what we can discover?"

That would give me enough time to see what Dot and Rosie had cooked up. Then I could spend a bit of time reconvening with the others before I met Jake for dinner. "Sounds good. I can give you a ride down there."

"We would really appreciate that," Poppy said.

I dropped the two of them back off at the resort then texted Dot and Rosie to let them know I was just a few minutes away. I couldn't wait to see what they had been doing at Tom Kidd's place.

Chapter 14

"WHAT HAVE YOU GOT?" I ASKED WHEN ROSIE opened the door for me at Dot's apartment. I walked in to find a black cat perched on the counter. She looked at me with her big yellow eyes then let out a loud meow.

"Middie would like you to know that she's starving to death, that she's never received a meal in her life, and that this must be remedied," Rosie announced.

"I can see that," I said, reaching over and stroking the black cat. Middie, whose full name was Threat Level: Midnight, was a stray abandoned by her former family who had lived in Rosie's building. When items began disappearing from people's apartments, we initially believed a person was responsible, but we eventually found the culprit was, in fact, the poor cat just trying to get food and attracted by shiny things.

Middie let out a contented meow.

"I've started bringing her to new places," Rosie explained. "I want her to be comfortable in new environments, especially as I train her."

"Train her?" I asked, raising an eyebrow.

"Oh, yes. I think a cat like Middie would be very useful to have in many situations. Cats are natural climbers; they can get in and out of places we could never think of."

"I think you've missed the part where cats are notoriously impossible to train."

Rosie scoffed. "Oh, please. That's a myth made up by people who can't be bothered taking the time and treats required to do it properly. They see a dog and think that's much easier to train, but having a cat who will do what you want can be so much more useful. Look at this: Middie, beg."

Middie immediately rolled onto her back, looking up at Rosie expectantly, her paws dangling adorably in front of her.

"Good girl," Rosie said happily, reaching into her pocket and pulling out a tiny treat, which she gave to Middie.

The cat noisily crunched her reward happily, while I shook my head, incredulous.

"Every day, I find new reasons to be terrified of you," I said.

"Well, Tom Kidd isn't nearly scared enough," Dot interrupted, spinning around on her chair at the computer to face us.

"Yeah, what were the two of you up to over there, anyway?" I asked. "You obviously got out okay."

"We did," Rosie confirmed.

"I wanted to get into his office while you were interviewing him," Dot said. "I tried to hack him remotely, and I did manage to get into one of his computers, but I had a sneaking suspicion it wasn't his main machine. There wasn't any of the good stuff on it. The stuff he uses to blackmail people. I figured he must physically move it to an air-gapped machine."

"Air-gapped?" I asked.

"A computer that has never been connected to the internet. The storage would have had to be moved physically, with a thumb drive. It's more secure when you've got information you cannot have get out. I suspected that Tom was finding the information on people then keeping it on an air-gapped computer for safety until he released it, which meant I needed to have physical access to his office."

"That makes sense," I agreed.

"It seemed like an ideal time to do it, while he would be distracted with you. Because the thing is, in looking at Tom Kidd, something wasn't adding up. There was a pattern. He was getting sued, yes, which you expect for someone who lives his life as a shock jock. But I was pretty sure he was getting access to information he shouldn't have had."

"When I was talking to him, he mentioned a woman running for mayor in California. He reported that she had cheated on her taxes, and she said that he couldn't have had access to that."

"Precisely," Dot said. "That was a case I looked at as well. As it turns out, she hadn't done anything wrong at all. She certainly wasn't committing tax evasion. Her accountant had messed up when he filed, it was noticed before the IRS looked at the taxes, and they issued a correction. It was all entirely by the book. The changes were filed, the IRS determined that she had done everything correctly, and no penalty was assessed."

"Tom essentially invented a controversy meant to disqualify her from winning the mayoral race," I said.

"He did," Dot replied. "And that is, in fact, part of his business plan. He knows he's going to get sued. He's well aware of it. He specifically makes claims that lead to lawsuits, but it's all part of the business for him."

"The controversy he generates brings in more money than what he spends on lawyers and settlements," I said.

"Exactly. But here is what I found interesting: in this specific case, which is one of the few that went to trial and wasn't settled out of court, the woman complained that Tom Kidd shouldn't have been able to get the data. She had no idea where he found out about the initial filing. She said the only people that knew were her, her husband, and her accountant."

"You started wondering if something else was going on."

"Yes. Something much less legal. Men like Tom Kidd, they don't recognize boundaries, and that includes the law. They think the world is theirs for the taking, and when I saw that, I began to wonder. I knew I needed to get into his office. To get into his computer and his files. I wondered what else he had. The computer I hacked into was all aboveboard. But nothing about Tom Kidd screams 'aboveboard' otherwise. There had to be more."

"And that's when you got the idea of breaking into his place while I was interviewing and having a look around."

Dot laughed. "That's right. I didn't expect his assistant to come in. She didn't see me; I heard her coming down the hall and was able to get out of sight. But of course, she spotted the glass on the ground from the window I'd broken."

"Wouldn't Kidd have a security system?"

Dot shot me a look that told me I should know better than to assume she wouldn't have disabled it before entering.

"Sorry. So, what did you find?" I asked.

"I'm going through it now. There are a lot of files on people he's mentioned on his show. And I don't think they were all obtained legally. In fact,

I'm sure they weren't. There are massive amounts of fraud happening here."

"Can you prove it?"

Dot stuck the tip of her tongue out of the corner of her mouth. "That's the problem. I'm not sure yet. But I do know one thing: he needs to be stopped. He's taking advantage of people. He's committing crimes and making millions of dollars in the process. He's making the world actively worse, and if he can be stopped, we need to do it."

"I agree. And I think Ophelia and Poppy will help us. I ran into them again, and we interviewed Janice together. They're not fans of his either. I organized to go meet them at the resort later."

"We'll see," Dot said. "I'm not a big fan of involving more people."

"Ophelia can be trusted," Rosie said. "I have that on extremely good authority. We'll go meet them, as planned. Do we have an idea about how we're going to trap Tom Kidd? And what the long game is? He deserves jail, but is that everything? And what if we can't prove beyond a reasonable doubt what he's doing? What does the plan become then?"

I bit my lower lip as I considered my answer. "That's a good question. We could use Becky as bait, somehow. He knows her. I think that could be one way of getting in."

"It can't be us," Rosie said. "As much as I'd love to be involved, our voices do sound a little bit older than what we're after. Tom Kidd wouldn't care what old ladies think of him."

"Vesper would be good. She's more than unhinged enough, but she's got the same problem. The decades of smoking have given her too much of a raspy voice. But that's why I think we should involve Poppy and Ophelia. I bet Poppy would be good at this."

My phone binged then, and I checked it to find a text from Jake.

Have to take a rain check on dinner, sorry. Something at work came up. A new case.

They're giving you new cases to work in the middle of this bombing?

Unfortunately. Make it tomorrow instead?

Done. Good luck!

Thanks. Someone carjacked two people and robbed a local store. I guess they thought they'd take advantage of the chaos.

I hope you find them.

"My schedule just opened up. My dinner plans are off; Jake just got assigned another case. Robbery and carjacking. Let me text Ophelia and see if they're up for this."

Hey, Ophelia. We're thinking of doing something like a fake podcast that's going to drive Tom Kidd into a mad frenzy. Are you in? It's for a good cause, I promise.

Her response came through a minute later. *I can't imagine anything we'd rather be involved in. Come by whenever you'd like.*

I grinned. "As it turns out, it's not actually hard to get people to help you if you tell them you're going to try and fuck with Tom Kidd."

Dot chuckled. "Why am I not surprised? Okay, I want to dig deeper into the files I stole off his computer. See if I can find something that will definitely get him sent to jail."

"We'll go down to the resort and meet you there, okay?"

"Perfect. I'll let you know what I find."

I gave Dot the details, and Rosie and I left the apartment building and hopped into Queenie.

"What's your instinct on these women?" Rosie asked. "You've met them, not me."

"Ophelia is whip quick. She knew I'd spent a lot of time in Washington State."

"It's because you still say 'pop' instead of 'soda.'"

"Seriously? You too?"

Rosie shrugged. "It's an easy way to know what region of America people are from."

"You're both as weird as each other."

"I'm going to take that as a compliment."

"It was meant as one, but also, I didn't realize my whole life was such an open book."

"It isn't. Don't worry. I'm just very good at what I do."

"Right. Well, Ophelia is very good at it too. So, be careful around her, obviously. Poppy is a lot more... I guess 'normal' is probably the right word for it."

"It would be nice to know exactly what we're getting into, but if you haven't gathered that intel then, so be it," Rosie said.

"Maybe avoid using phrases like 'gathering intel' in front of Ophelia," I suggested.

Rosie glanced at me out of the corner of her eye. "I've been keeping my identity secret since before your mother was born."

"Okay, okay, fair enough," I replied with a chuckle.

We reached the parking lot for the Maui Diamond resort then headed inside. As we walked past the front desk and toward the elevators, I overheard a man arguing with a member of the staff.

"What do you mean, La Mer is still closed? I made my reservation months ago. Do you know how hard it was to get?"

"I understand, sir," the poor employee on the other side of the desk replied in a much, much calmer voice than the one I would have used. "But the restaurant is still a crime scene. The police haven't given us permission to enter, and after that we'll have to see what kind of damage has been caused before we're able to reopen."

"That's bullshit," the man replied, stomping his feet. "I planned this whole holiday around La Mer."

"I'm very sorry to hear that. We have four other restaurants on the premises that are just as..."

"No! I booked La Mer. I want La Mer."

We moved past the desk and out of hearing range of the rest of the conversation, but I turned and shot Rosie a "yikes" look.

"Some people really need to gain perspective and realize their holiday is not the only thing that's important in a situation where five people lost their lives," Rosie said, shaking her head.

As we reached the elevators, my eyes were drawn to the pile of newspapers on the stand in between them. Today's edition of the *New York Times* sat on top.

"No Arrests Yet in Hawaii Bombing," the headline read in large letters. Below was an image—half below the fold that I couldn't make out—showing the back of La Mer in the immediate aftermath of the bombing. A tearful woman in the photograph's foreground held her head in her hands while smoke still rose from the burnt remains of the palm tree that had caught on fire.

I tore my eyes away and entered the elevator. The best way we could help was to get answers, and fast.

Poppy answered the door of what turned out to be one of the penthouse suites at the Maui Diamond. I tried not to look astounded as we were led into a living room the size of a tennis court. Ophelia was at the large desk, tapping away on the computer, and on the couch was another woman I hadn't met.

Tall and slim, with black hair tied back into a high braid, she wore a short, tropical skirt and a pair of chunky sandals with a form-fitting black tank top. She held iced coffee from Honolulu Coffee Company in one hand and the remote in the other.

Her dark eyes glanced at us as she walked in. "So, you're the other investigator that has these two all in a tizzy," she said, not making any motion to get up.

"This is Taylor," Poppy said, motioning toward her. "She works with us when she can, but mostly she's just here for the beach. According to her."

"I have a very special set of skills, and they don't involve interviewing boring people who have been victims of crime," Taylor replied, her eyes turning back to the television. She was watching one of those bad martial arts movies from the nineties, the kind with a budget of half a pack of gum and whatever the producers found under the couch cushions, and she seemed completely engrossed by it.

"Your skills might come in handy now," Ophelia said, turning from her computer and looking at us. "This case appears to involve Tom Kidd, and he's not going to be pleased when he finds out he's on my radar."

Taylor cackled. "Good. There's not many people in this world who deserve to get taken down more than him. What are you going to do? Have him arrested?"

"We're hoping to find proof he's committed

crimes, but he's good. He's connected, he's rich, and he's powerful. And he knows what he's doing."

"And he's got the living armor of being a white man," Taylor finished.

"We found evidence that he is gathering information he shouldn't have on people, but as you know, being aware of something as a fact and being able to prove it in a court of law are two different things," Rosie said to Ophelia.

"Poppy, Ophelia, Taylor, this is Rosie," I said, introducing her.

"It's nice to meet you," Ophelia said. "And you're one hundred percent correct. People like Tom Kidd are careful. It's the reason they haven't been caught before. If we're going to do this, we have to draw him out. He's hiding in his nest, and we need him to come out so we can pounce."

"Oh, that's easy," Taylor said, her gaze not leaving the TV screen. We all looked at her.

"Enlighten us?" Poppy asked.

"You make fun of him."

"Make fun of him how?"

"The thing about men like Tom Kidd is that they think they're these macho, alpha Arnie-types. They want everyone to believe they're big and strong and that they're the hero of an action movie. But they're not. They're actually fragile man-babies who would piss their pants if they ever got into a *real* life-or-death situation."

I nodded. "Totally. When I was interviewing

Tom and Lisa mentioned an intruder, he fled to his panic room faster than Coco when she hears me say the word "bath"."

"Exactly," Taylor agreed. "And one thing these men are more scared of than anything is people making them look like idiots. They don't want to be laughed at. It bruises their ego. Because *real* men, in their mind, aren't laughed at. They're revered. Respected. Like kings. It's really fucked up, but there you go."

"She's right, though," I said. "The best way to annoy a guy like that is to laugh at him. And if we can make the whole world laugh at him, that's going to drive him insane. And he might do something stupid then."

"I have a friend who can help," Taylor said. "She runs a social media empire based on mocking misogynistic dudes on the internet. I don't think she's ever gone after Tom Kidd before."

"And we have the perfect footage for her to use," I said with a grin. "I was recording the conversation I had with Kidd, just in case. We have live footage of him hearing about the intruder and running away."

Taylor snapped her fingers and grabbed her phone that had been sitting face-down on the armchair next to her. "Perfect. I'll text her now. We're going to ruin this man's life."

I had no way to stop the grin spreading across my face. I couldn't wait.

Chapter 15

WHILE TAYLOR TEXTED, OPHELIA GAVE ME A HARD look. "If we do this and use that footage, Kidd will know where it came from. He's going to come after you."

"I've had worse than him try," I said, the words causing a slight lurch in my stomach. Weeks had passed since Brady Ludlam, an associate of the Ham brothers, had been arrested on the island with a block of cocaine I'd planted in his car—along with a message to the Seattle gangsters to leave me alone, or I would make them pay.

Brady was rotting away in jail while he awaited trial, and although no other known Ham brothers associates had come to the island yet, I knew he had spoken to them over the phone. Dot and Rosie were keeping an eye on his communications for me so we wouldn't be surprised if they tried anything.

Had Brady passed on the message? Were they

going to decide enough was enough and let me live my life in peace? Or was I just waiting for the notification from Dot that the Ham brothers had gotten on a plane, and was I going to have to deal with them then?

I had no idea yet, but it was a hell of a sword of Damocles hanging over me.

"I'll get Dot to forward us the footage," Rosie said, pulling out her own phone.

Taylor's binged a moment later. "Hayley's in."

"Who's your friend?" Poppy asked.

"Hayley Yarrow."

"Oh, I've heard of her," I said. "I've seen some of her videos. She finds videos online of men bullying women then posts her replies making fun of them. And they can't handle it."

"Exactly," Taylor replied, grinning. "That's the beauty of it. She's doing to them what they're doing, but because they're toxic as hell, they melt down instead of taking what they dole out to other people like adults. And Tom Kidd is going to be the perfect target."

"It isn't enough to create a funny video, however," Ophelia pointed out. "If the goal is to entrap him into committing a crime, we have to be prepared."

"We do," Rosie said. "And I know exactly what needs to be done. Kidd will come after Charlie if this video is posted—her false identity as Becky, anyway—and if we play our cards right, we can prove it. We can gather evidence of him committing his crime and have him locked up for good."

"Plus, the video of him running away from a suspected intruder is going to make him look like an idiot to all of his followers," I said. "He's always going on about how a big, strong man protects his family and how he's an alpha male and the head of the pack. That doesn't work so well when you look like a startled antelope at the first sign of trouble."

"Exactly," Ophelia said. "So we do this. We fool him into committing a crime on camera, and as an added bonus, we get him to be the laughingstock of the internet for a little while. He goes to jail and looks like an idiot in the process. That is our best-case scenario. I am certain it will not convince all his listeners to abandon him."

"But I also doubt Halawa will let him bring his recording equipment in so he can broadcast live from the yard," Rosie finished.

"Precisely. We need to get him off the air, and the best way to do that is jail."

"He's going to be so angry when he finds out a bunch of women did this to him," Taylor said, cackling maniacally.

I couldn't agree more.

THE FOUR OF US SET TO WORK PLANNING OUR TRAP. A lot of moving parts were involved; we had to set up a fake address for Becky and put it out there on the internet so that Tom Kidd would be able to find it. Then, we had to rig the whole place up with cameras.

We figured Tom would practice his usual M.O.: breaking into the home, finding files on the computer—data, papers, anything that would show Becky doing something she shouldn't—and revealing them online.

Dot handled all the technical stuff from her apartment, while Ophelia set about creating fake documents to plant inside "Becky's" home. I reached out to a few friends and found out from Zoe that one of the doctors at the hospital was away for a couple of weeks visiting family on the mainland. He was happy to let us use his apartment without asking too many questions.

Taylor, Poppy and I worked on the perfect script to help drive Tom Kidd bonkers, with Hayley Yarrow joining us on a video call from her home in New York City.

"Every word counts," Poppy explained as we got started. "Every single word. We have to make sure we hit him where he's most insecure. You know when you go to therapy, and they tell you something that really hits you in the gut?"

"No, I don't go to therapy," Taylor replied.

"You need to see a shrink more than anyone else I've ever met," Poppy told her.

"I don't go, either, and my best friend has said the same thing," I chimed in.

Taylor reached across the table and gave me a high five, while Poppy shook her head at us.

"Look, every word counts. You're right. We need him to get completely unhinged when he sees this," Taylor agreed. "We hit him right in the insecurities. He's going to lose it."

It took us four hours to come up with a script that everyone agreed was perfect. Hayley promised to have it recorded within the hour and would hang onto it until the morning, when we agreed to post it. That would give Dot the whole night to leave enough computer equipment and files in the doctor's home and set up all the security.

By the time we were getting ready to leave, it was nearly nine o'clock.

"I'm impressed you have someone proficient enough with computers to handle all of this," Ophelia said. "We have a woman on our team who specializes in that, but she couldn't leave the city."

"Ours is better anyway," I replied with a wink.

"Oh, I don't know about that," Poppy said.

I smiled at her in reply, but I knew Dot was better than anybody in the world at this stuff.

"We'll meet back here first thing in the morning," Rosie said. "We have a big day ahead of us tomorrow."

I nodded. "And we still have to find who set off that bomb. Who knows? Maybe Tom Kidd left it there himself. Maybe that's why he asked to change tables—so he wouldn't be in the blast radius but could still claim it was him."

"Now there's an interesting idea," Ophelia said quietly. "You're right. We will look at this case again in the morning. We will see you soon."

Rosie and I left and went back to Queenie.

"What did you think of them?" I asked.

"Your assessment was correct. Ophelia is incredibly intelligent. She doesn't miss anything."

"It's too bad they don't live on the island; I think we'd all be good friends."

"Yes, I think so too," Rosie agreed. "I think so too."

I DROPPED HER BACK OFF AT DOT'S SO SHE COULD continue working with her and pick up Middie, and I headed home and found Zoe in the kitchen.

"How's it going?" I asked.

"It's good. I just woke up. It's been busy."

"I know. I'm working the case."

"Good. That night was one of the most insane things I've ever seen in the hospital. It was all hands on deck."

"I can only imagine."

"We're not set up for that kind of disaster. This sort of thing doesn't happen here. It was awful."

I joined her at the dining table, where Zoe was

eating a bagel. Coco was ignoring me; her energy was entirely devoted to trying to use the Force to convince Zoe to drop a piece of bagel onto the ground. Or maybe just a little clump of cream cheese.

"I had some of the pie that was dropped off," Zoe said. "I assume that was you?"

I grinned. "Sure was. The woman working the counter added a couple to the order when she learned what they were for, so it was a joint effort."

"It was really nice. Thank you."

"Hey, it's the least I could do. I saw the damage."

"Do you know who did it yet?"

I shook my head. "No. I'm hoping to figure it out soon."

"And is Jake okay with all of this?"

"He's been surprisingly supportive this time around."

"Surprisingly?"

"Well, you know how he can be."

"I know how you can be too. You blame him, but you're both responsible for how this goes."

"No, it's his fault if he can't handle me doing this work."

"But it's your fault when you push in beyond what is reasonable and try to convince him to give you unfettered access to a police investigation."

"No, that's also his fault."

Zoe shot me a look that said everything it needed to. "What are you up to tonight, then?"

I paused and looked at the clock. It was nine thirty. "I was thinking of driving up to Mom's place."

"Saying hi?"

I shifted uncomfortably in my chair. "No. I just kind of want to see what she's up to, you know?"

Zoe raised an eyebrow. "You're stalking your own mother?"

"It's not stalking."

"You're going to go to her house and watch what she does from your car. That's stalking."

"I'm a private investigator. That's what I do."

"And who hired you to follow your own mother?"

"No one," I admitted.

"Yeah, that's called stalking. Why are you doing it to your own mother?"

"She saw a lawyer the other day."

"By that logic, I should look out for cameras you've snuck into the living room, because so did I."

"Okay, two things. One, your mom is a lawyer. That doesn't count. You weren't seeing a lawyer because you needed legal work. And two, she lied to me about it after."

Zoe's eyebrows twitched slightly. "Oh? Okay, that's interesting. How do you know?"

"She called me and said she put Jake in her will."

Zoe did a spit take. "She *what?*"

"Yeah. And normally, my mom weirdly trying to push my relationships forward doesn't stand out as exceptional. But I'm not married, and Mom would *never* do that without making sure I got a ring on that finger first."

"I agree. That doesn't sound like Carmen at all."

"And on top of that, when she was telling me, she was being cagey about it. I know my mom. She's a bad liar. And she was lying to me."

"What about?"

"I don't know. Hence the stakeout."

"Stalking."

"Po-tay-to, po-tah-to."

"Not the same thing at all."

"Okay, but like, something weird is going on, and I want to know what."

"Have you considered asking your mother? You know, like a normal human being would do?"

I snorted. "No. She wouldn't tell me if I asked her anyway. You know what she's like."

"Right. The person who's about to stalk her own mother is definitely the one who should be criticizing other people right now," Zoe shot back.

"Fine, well, I was going to ask if you wanted to come with. But I guess not."

"Oh, no, I'm definitely coming. This is going to backfire on you somehow, and when it does, I want to see it."

"That's a terrible reason, and you're uninvited."

"If you don't let me come, I'm going to text your mother to look outside and see you sitting in your Jeep, which is the least inconspicuous vehicle on this whole island."

"It's also the snazziest," I pointed out.

"Didn't say it wasn't. But astronauts can see it from space. Your mother is going to see it from her living room."

"Okay, good point. Fine, you're re-invited, but we have to take your car."

"I guess so. When do you want to leave?"

"How long do you need? Probably sooner rather than later? Mom normally goes to bed around eleven, so if anything's going on with her, it'll be before then. We probably won't even see anything. She'll just be watching Colbert, and when the guests come on, she'll turn the TV off and go to sleep."

Zoe nodded and took a big sip to finish off her coffee. "I'm good to go now. I just got up. My next shift doesn't start until two, so we can do this for a few hours until then. It'll be nice to catch up too."

I smiled at my friend. "I agree."

"Then, when there's a completely normal explanation for the way your mom's been acting, you can tell me I was right."

"Not going to happen," I replied as I grabbed Coco's leash to take her out quickly before we left. "I know it. Mom is up to something. I just need to find out what."

Chapter 16

T EN MINUTES LATER, WE WERE ON THE ROAD. W E stopped at the twenty-four-hour Texaco for snacks, then Zoe drove up the back roads to my mom's place, where she did a slow drive-by of Mom's house before making a U-turn and parking two houses away.

I frowned, growing suspicious. "She's not home."

Picking up on the tone of my voice, Zoe turned and looked at me. "She's a grown woman, Charlie. There are plenty of reasons why your mom might not be home right now."

I shook my head. "There are not. I know my mom. She's like a wild rabbit. Once the sun goes down, she heads to her burrow, and she stays there until the morning, drinking a glass of wine and watching her shows. She's not the kind to be out after nine o'clock."

"Maybe she ran out of wine and ran down to the store to get some more," Zoe suggested. "There are a million reasonable explanations. Come on, eat some chips, drink some of your iced tea, and tell me about your case while we wait for Carmen to come home so you can overthink everything a bit more."

Zoe reached into the bag and pulled out salt and vinegar chips, which she knew were my favourite, and handed them to me along with my Arizona Iced Tea. The best part about a good stakeout was the snacks.

This wasn't stalking. No one ever took snacks to stalk someone. Take that, Zoe.

I grabbed a couple of chips, ate them, then started telling Zoe all about the case. I ran through meeting Ophelia, Poppy, and Taylor and devising our new plan and had just about gotten to the end of the story when a set of headlights filled my view.

"Duck," I ordered, stopping my story in mid-sentence.

The two of us crouched down low in our seats, and I watched the car then glanced at my phone. Nearly twenty minutes had passed since we'd gotten here, and it was almost ten thirty.

Honestly, a part of me expected the car to keep driving past, going on to another property, but when it turned into Mom's driveway, I gasped.

"That's not her car!"

"Maybe she's getting a ride home from something with someone."

The porch light offered just enough illumination for me to make out what was happening. The car in the driveway was a dark sedan, newer than Mom's. She got out of the passenger seat, and I began to wonder if maybe Zoe was right, when the driver climbed out too.

"That's a man!" I practically shouted, pointing at him.

Next to me in the driver's seat, Zoe started laughing uncontrollably.

"It's not funny," I snapped as I leaned forward, trying to get a better view of him.

He climbed out of the car and walked over to the passenger side, where he reached over and slipped an arm around Mom's waist. I audibly gasped when I saw the scene.

She looked up and smiled at him as the two of them walked toward the front door, the porch light shining on their faces.

I finally got a decent look at him. He was older, his black hair mixed in with a few streaks of white around the temples. He was of medium height and medium build, only a few inches taller than Mom.

"She's going to invite him in," I spluttered, rubbing my eyes to make sure I was seeing properly.

"Of course she is," Zoe said. "They're obviously a couple."

"This can't be happening. This is the worst thing that has ever happened to me."

"It's very funny, actually."

I turned and glared at her. "It is not. What's funny about it?"

"You decided to stalk your mother, and this is how you find out she's dating again, and now you're melting down about it."

"I'm not stalking."

"You are too."

"Well, if I'm stalking, then so are you."

"Nope."

"What do you call this, then?" I asked, motioning around.

"Babysitting."

I stuck my tongue out at her. "I don't have time for your witty comebacks. My mom is dating someone, Zoe. What should we do? Should we go in there?"

"Yes, you're definitely the kind of person who would handle walking in on your mom having sex with the mature and levelheaded attitude of someone who's basically in her thirties."

I gasped. "Sex?"

"Yes, Charlie. Look at them. That's what comes next."

I let out a groan and slunk into my seat. I felt like my world was spinning. What was even happening? Mom, dating? No way. This wasn't a thing. This couldn't be a thing. Mom didn't date. She had never. Not since Dad died.

Zoe pulled out her phone and began tapping

away. "Yeah, that explains this. Here he is. Lucas Aoki. He works as a lawyer, focusing on contract law, up in Kahului."

"That's why she was being so weird. She didn't want me to know she was seeing someone who wanted to show her his briefs."

Zoe snickered. "That's certainly one way of phrasing that."

"Oh God, Zoe, what do I do?"

"About this? Nothing. You let your mom date a guy she obviously likes. Although you can tell me I was right, as I predicted."

"What if he ends up being a serial killer?"

"While that's definitely a reasonable place for your brain to go right off the bat, you don't assume that for now. You haven't met him. You haven't seen any red flags, and there are no known serial killers on the island."

"'Known' is doing a lot of work in that sentence," I pointed out.

"What's really bugging you about this? Is it the fact that your mom is seeing someone who isn't your dad?"

I curled in on myself in the front seat a little bit, like a sulking child. "No."

"Then what is it?"

"I don't know," I admitted broodily. "I guess... it's just weird, okay? It's different. It's Mom. She's been single forever. I guess I thought she would never date again. Not that I think she shouldn't. Just, she didn't seem like the type. And now I see this…"

"Okay, and you think?" Zoe prompted.

"I guess I wonder if this is the first time she's dated. Mom is too old to date."

Zoe's eyebrows rose. "I'd love to hear the reasoning behind that."

"I don't have any," I grumbled. "I just… I don't know. It's different. It's different and I hate it."

"For now, why don't we go home? Let your mom have her nice night with her boyfriend."

"Why wouldn't she tell me about it?" I interrupted.

Zoe shrugged. "You'd have to ask her. But there are plenty of reasons why she might not want you to know. Maybe their relationship is new, and she doesn't want to get you involved when she's not sure if it's going to go anywhere. Maybe she's worried you'd freak out."

"Don't know why she'd think that," I muttered.

"Yes, that she acted slightly out of the ordinary one time and then you decided to stalk her shows that you're very good at handling this sort of thing like an adult."

"Look," I started, but I had nothing. Zoe was right. As always.

"She knows how much you loved your dad," Zoe continued quietly. "Maybe she didn't want you thinking that she was betraying him somehow by dating again. Do you think that?"

I sighed. "No. At least, not really. Maybe there's a part of me deep down that kind of thinks that, but I know it's not really the case. Dad died fifteen years ago. He would have wanted, more than anything, for Mom to be happy. And if that meant finding someone else to spend her life with, then Dad would have wanted that."

"It's normal to feel a lot of emotions when you get some big news like this. You have to process what you've just found out."

"Does processing involve eating more chips?" I asked, reaching for the bag at my feet and grabbing another packet of salt and vinegar.

"For you? Always," Zoe replied with a smile as she started the car and pulled away. "I promise, Charlie, it's going to be fine."

"Spoken like someone who didn't just see a lawyer go into maritime law."

"What?"

"He's obviously got some seamen he needs released."

Zoe snorted. "Oh my God."

"If mom is going to date a lawyer, I am coming up with a whole list of these."

She shot me a smile. "I knew you'd be fine."

We pulled back into the parking lot at our place, and Zoe turned off the car.

"Sorry for melting down back there," I said, not making a move for my seat belt.

Zoe reached a hand across the center console and placed it on mine. "You don't have to apologize. It was a big thing to see, for you. You didn't know your mom was dating. You didn't know what was going on. It was normal to have questions, and your response is your own. I'm just glad you didn't barge in there and see something that would have burned an image onto your retinas that you could never unsee."

"I think we're all glad for that. Thanks for babysitting."

"You're welcome. What are friends for?"

I squeezed her hand. "I'm not sure everyone has a friend who will come out in the middle of the night with her to stake out her own mother's house because she got a weird phone call."

"You mean stalk, and I've been friends with you for long enough to know this is par for the course," Zoe replied. "Now come on. You've had a big day, and I have to get to work. Let's go inside. You can get some sleep, and in the morning, you'll feel better."

"Have I ever told you I love you, Zoe?" I asked as I climbed out of the car.

"Here and there," she replied.

The two of us went back inside, and I immediately collapsed on the bed. It had been a huge day, and even though my mind was racing with thoughts, it didn't take long before the exhaustion of the day's events took me over and I fell into a deep sleep.

It was a good thing too. Tomorrow was going to be a big day. We were baiting the hook, and I hoped we were going to catch ourselves a big, bottom-feeding fish.

Chapter 17

I woke up to the alarm on my phone just after six, groaned, mashed at the screen until the device stopped screaming at me, then rolled out of bed and sat on the floor while trying to rub the sleep out of my eyes and feel human again.

This was going to be the kind of day when "drinking" meant "pounding a Red Bull and following it with a shot of espresso as a chaser."

I headed into the kitchen, turned on the coffee maker, and fed Coco, who jumped up on me to let me know The Force hadn't worked last night and Zoe didn't drop half a bagel for her, so now she was starving to death.

When she was finished inhaling her food, I grabbed a mug of coffee and walked down to the beach with Coco so she could get a bit of exercise in on those little legs. It was still dark out, and I used the flashlight on my phone to make sure I didn't trip over a sleeping *honu*, but Coco didn't seem to have any problems with the dimness. As we reached the beach, the first hint of light peeked over from behind the mountain, and it didn't take long before the clouds dotting the sky took on a pink hue, in beautiful contrast to the azure sky above.

I pulled out my phone and sent Jake a text. On a case like this, he would be up this early, too. If he'd gone to bed at all.

How's the case going for you?

He replied a minute later. *Frustrating. Not getting far, to be honest. There are a lot of moving parts here. We're leaning toward the idea that Tom Kidd's group was the target. The timeline doesn't make much sense otherwise.*

The corners of my mouth curled up into a smile. Jake had come to the same conclusion as we had. *That's what I'm thinking too. It makes the most sense. How's the other case going? The robberies?*

We have some leads on that. Splitting time between the two, but it's tough. Lots to do here today. Chat to you later?

You got it. We're busy here too. Hoping to figure out who the killer was by tonight, though. We'll see.

Stay safe.

You too.

I tucked my phone away then called Coco over; she ran back with a stick in her mouth that probably weighed twice what she did and insisted on carrying it all the way back to the apartment. Even though it meant I would come home tonight to a living room rug covered in wood scraps, I couldn't let her leave it outside after she'd put all that effort into lugging it back with her.

So I left her inside with the stick then hopped into Queenie. After I picked up Dot and then Rosie, the three of us drove down to the Maui Diamond resort, where we were going to put our plan into action.

Hayley Yarrow was supposed to have posted the video at six o'clock Hawaii time, which was eleven o'clock Eastern. Hayley had assured us that according to her analytics, that would get the most views throughout the day, and it would also allow the news stations on the East Coast to report on it in time for the evening news.

She was sure this video was going to blow up, and she was right.

Poppy immediately ushered the three of us into the room by when we arrived. "It's already happening," she announced happily. "Hayley posted the video, and it's up to a million views on TikTok. Half a mill on Instagram."

My eyes widened. "Already?"

"Never discount how much people desperately want to see someone shitty get absolutely wrecked publicly," Taylor called out. She was getting up. "I'm going for a coffee run, so put your orders in. Just a heads up, I refuse to order anything hot. It's iced coffee or nothing."

"A woman after my own heart," I said with a smile.

"Let's see the final product," Dot insisted.

I pulled out my phone while Taylor grabbed coffee orders. I connected the phone to the television then opened up TikTok and typed "Hayley Yarrow" in the search bar. A moment later I had her account and pressed Play on the most recent video.

It began with Hayley on the screen, sitting in the front seat of a car. She looked to be around my age, maybe a couple of years younger. Her auburn hair was curly and long, reaching well past her shoulders and out of frame of the video. Her big brown eyes were eclipsed by her large mouth, covered in bright red lipstick that didn't look overdone against her tanned skin.

"Hi everyone," she said in a sing-song voice. "It's your girl, Hayley, and boy, have I got a video for you today. You're going to want to sit down for this one, because it's a doozy. Now, we all know this guy."

The screen switched to a clip of Tom Kidd. He was sitting inside a studio, with a professional microphone on the desk in front of him and a notepad and pen next to him. He was wearing a dark-blue button-down shirt and his trademark knit cap. Across from him, just barely in the screen, was a man he was interviewing, also set up with a microphone. But the camera was focused on Tom, who leaned forward as he started talking.

"Now here's this thing we were talking about

before, Zach," Tom said. "You know these women who go out to events, and they put on Spanx. Or other stuff like it. Anything that's designed to make them look thinner. You know what I think? That's fraud. Because what happens is you see a beautiful woman, and you decide you want to take her home. You flirt for a bit, you throw on that alpha-male charm, and the next thing you know, she's begging you to get out of there and find somewhere a bit more private, if you know what I mean."

I rolled my eyes and released an audible sound of disgust. Tom sounded like a guy whose only experience in picking up women came from reading Reddit posts on the topic.

He continued. "But here's the thing. You get there, and you start undressing her, and when you take that off you realize that hot, slim thing you saw at the party is actually part sea lion. That's fucking fraud, man."

The man Tom was speaking to started laughing, but the video cut straight back to Hayley, who burst out laughing herself.

"Okay, okay," she said, holding up her hands. "First things first, let's not pretend it's only women that do this. But you know the difference? We can fucking tell ahead of time what you're hiding, because you're not subtle, you potato with eyes. Do you think you're really fooling people with the whole ski cap thing? Do you think we genuinely believe you wear it all the time because it makes you look cool? Because here's a fun fact for you, human dish-cloth. We are *well* aware your hairline ran away from you faster than your dad when he promised he was just going out for cigarettes. You're not fooling anyone. She's long gone, baby. It's like a twenty-dollar cab ride from your eyebrows to your hairline. I bet you dream in IMAX, don't you? Here's an idea: you could run a side hustle offering parking on that bitch."

Hayley cackled, and I was glad Taylor hadn't come back with the coffee yet because I would have definitely done a spit-take.

"But here's the thing. I don't actually *care* about the fact that *Coneheads* was a documentary about your family. Because unlike you, I don't judge a person entirely by how hot they are, because I'm not fourteen years old anymore. But what I do judge is what a person says. We all know you love MMA, Tom. Want to tell us about that, for the millionth time?"

Hayley put her chin on her fist and grinned to the camera as it cut away to yet another clip of Tom. The camera was in the same spot, but the guest was different.

"You know me, Kevin. I'm really big into MMA. Could have gone pro, if I wanted to. But God put me on this earth for another reason. To save America. And that's what I'm doing. But here's the thing: When you're an alpha male, you protect your family. You protect your people. You protect yourself. America, when we're at war, we're just protecting ourselves. Protecting our values. But if someone comes after me, you bet your ass I'm going to take them on. I'm not going to run away. They tell you to run, to stay safe. No. That's bullshit. A real man fights. He holds his ground. And he takes on his enemies, no matter how many of them there are."

The camera cut back to Hayley. The smile across her face was so huge, so genuine, I knew she was enjoying this.

"Hey, Tom, this you?" she asked.

The camera cut away again, and this time I recognized the scene. It was taken from the camera Dot had given me before the meeting with Tom Kidd. That camera was hidden in the button of my shirt just to be safe. We had no idea at the time how handy it would be.

I turned, and the camera focused on Lisa, her face pale, her hands trembling as she held the box in front of her. "There's an intruder. There was glass on the floor. Someone's here."

Tom jumped to his feet, and I turned, the camera going with me. The look of fear on his face was obvious. "Call security and the police. I'll be in the panic room."

He sprinted out of the room, and the shot cut back to Hayley.

She began laughing maniacally, like it was the funniest thing she'd ever seen. "That wasn't very *alpha male* of you now, was it, Tom? Is that you, running out of there faster than a guy who just ate three-day-old fast food that's been sitting on the counter? Now, I want to thank my friend Becky Byrd for getting this marvelous footage. Because ultimately, we know you were lying about more than just your hairline, Tom. And now everyone else can see it too. But hey, pity about that MMA career. I'm sure it would have gone real well for you."

Hayley let out another cackle, then the video ended.

For a couple of seconds, the room was silent. Then I laughed. "That's absolutely perfect."

"I think it will be very effective," Ophelia agreed.

"Hayley did good work. The editing is top-notch. She's really going to have made him angry," Dot said. "I'm impressed."

"We haven't finished," Rosie pointed out. "This is step one, and it's working. It's getting millions of views. But it also means we need to move forward with the rest of the plan. Charlie, we need to get you outside, take a picture of you, and post it to social media to show that you're not planning on being at 'home' today. Dot, how is the camera setup looking?"

"All ready to go. They're live and recording. I checked them as soon as I got up this morning. And I have a record of the files being available only on the air-gapped computer I left in the place. There's no other way they could have been accessed without being stolen."

"What did you put in there, out of curiosity?" I asked.

Dot flashed me a mischievous look. "I figured Kidd would want something he wouldn't be able to resist posting straight away. They're Photoshopped documents that make you look like you're a wanted criminal in fourteen states who ran away to Hawaii to avoid facing jail time."

"Cool. What crimes did you make me commit? They better be good crimes! Nothing boring. I would be a creative criminal."

"You ran an elaborate set of scams through a network of states, ultimately getting away with seventeen million dollars before changing your identity, dyeing your hair, and moving to Hawaii."

"Ooh, I like it," I said. "That sounds like a worthy crime."

"And as soon as he posts it, we're going to have evidence that he obtained it illegally, even if he himself doesn't do the dirty work of breaking into the fake home we've set up. Although I don't think it would be that difficult to prove a connection. We'll get him directly for the theft."

"How much jail time would he face in this state?"

"He's going to have to take the computer. I have that thing bricked up so well Trump would have begged me to use it for his wall with Mexico.

Unluckily for Kidd, I threw a bunch of jewelry into the case, which means when the police find it and open it, he'll have stolen a computer technically worth over twenty grand, making this a first-degree theft. That carries a term of ten years in prison."

Poppy shook her head, incredulous. "You all work *very* thoroughly."

Ophelia smiled. "I agree, and I approve of the plan entirely. Excellent job. He will undoubtedly fall into the trap, and by the end of the day, we should ideally have another person harming the world off the streets—and the airwaves—for a long time."

"Unfortunately, nature abhors a vacuum, and I am certain someone else will pop right on in and step into the hole Kidd will leave, but the video might convince some of his followers to look elsewhere for their life advice," Rosie said.

"That's fine with me, as long as this particular douchenozzle rots away at Halawa. Then we'll see just how much of an alpha male he really is," I said.

"Not to mention, if he was involved in the setting of the bomb as a publicity stunt, that will end him entirely," Ophelia said.

Taylor returned then, her arms laden with trays of coffee, and my phone binged in my pocket.

I just saw a video taken from the inside of Tom Kidd's place. There are no faces, but why do my Spidey senses tell me you're involved somehow?

I smiled as I typed out my reply. *You wouldn't let me come interview him with you, so…*

Every day I wake up and I ask myself what insane thing you're going to do today, and every day you manage to go so, so far beyond anything I could have ever dreamed up myself.

He deserves everything that's coming to him.

I agree entirely, but I'm also worried about your safety. A man like that, what you've just done, he's not going to take this lying down.

Don't worry. We have that covered.

I know. But if you need anything, let me know.

It's cool. We should be fine. But thanks. You've got two important cases going too.

No case is as important to me as your safety.

My insides twisted a little as I read those words. It was as if Jake had just enveloped me in a hug with his text message, and I relaxed just a little, knowing that above everything, he always had my back if I needed it.

How is the other one going?

Good. We've got a few leads that I hope are going to pan out later today. If we're lucky, we should have an arrest made in the next few hours. If you need anything, though—you tell me, I'm there.

Thanks. I'll let you know, but for now, I think you're good to keep going as if you hadn't seen that video.

Boy, am I glad I did, though. My only regret is that I wasn't in the room the first time he did too.

Same.

I'll talk to you later. Good luck. Stay safe. And CALL ME if you get into trouble.

I will. Bye.

I slipped the phone back into my pocket. This was better. This was improvement. Jake was actively talking to me about cases. He wasn't trying to get me to stop what I was doing, but he still showed he cared about me. I knew his history. I knew he was terrified that something would go wrong, but he was giving me the freedom that I needed to do my job.

"We are spiders, and we have laid our web. Now, we wait to see if our prey walks aimlessly into it," Ophelia said.

"That metaphor is insulting to flies' intelligence," I replied with a smile. "There's no way Tom Kidd avoids it."

Chapter 18

"Right," Dot said, pulling out a laptop and setting herself up at the massive dining table. "I'm going to be watching the security camera footage. I don't think it's going to be long before he finds it. I left a couple of bread crumbs through the internet last night with this address listed as Becky's, and I imagine it won't take long before he gets there."

"You can use my computer as well," Ophelia suggested.

"It's all right. I always carry a spare," Dot said, reaching into her bag and pulling out a second laptop.

I bit back a smile as she set it up.

"I want this one to keep an eye on the social media feeds," she said. "It's going to be important today to see who's talking about this. If anyone spots Kidd out in public, they're going to be recording it and uploading it to the internet."

"What do you need us to do?" Ophelia asked.

"Right now, you go back to finding out who set that bomb. I'll take care of everything here, and when we have the proof we need, we can give it to the police and confront him."

"Sounds like a plan," I said. "Although I'm starting to think Tom Kidd did this himself."

"If only there had been security footage taken from that table," Poppy mused. "That would make everything so much easier."

"Would it?" Ophelia asked. "I'm not certain. Are all the victims still in hospital?"

"I can find out," I replied.

It didn't take long for me to get our answer. Amir and Courtney were still in the hospital. Ed and Howard had both been patched up and discharged, and Julia had never been admitted at all, since she'd been in the bathroom when the bomb had gone off. Ed, Howard, and Julia were still checked into the hotel, and the group had decided to return to California together once the two patients still admitted to the hospital were finally released.

"I just asked the three who have been released, and they're willing to have breakfast with us," I said, taking a sip of my iced caramel latte. "We should do it. Amir thinks that Ed and Julia were having an affair. I'd like to see for myself whether or not that's true."

I organized for us to meet a few minutes later.

Dot, Rosie, and Taylor decided to stay upstairs—with Taylor claiming she didn't want to miss a single second of the drama happening on the internet—so Ophelia, Poppy, and I took the elevator downstairs.

We walked through the main concourse and to the other restaurant at the back of the hotel, simply called Ohana, the Hawaiian word for "family." This restaurant was more casual, with all-day service, starting with a breakfast buffet that overlooked the beach. Here, while the tables weren't covered with tablecloths, the tops were still made of sleek, glossy dark honey-colored wood. The matching chairs had wicker seats and backs. Palm-shaped fans spun lazily above, adding to the breeze coming in from the open windows, which gave a view over the ocean.

Letting the hostess know what group we were with, we were led to a large table near the window. Ed was already there, and as soon as he spotted us, he smiled and raised an arm in greeting, wincing with pain and clutching at his side as he did.

"Sorry. I keep forgetting how much it hurts when I move my right arm," he said apologetically as we all sat down. "I feel like a toddler who hasn't learned to keep their hand off the hot stove yet."

"It's normal. You've spent your whole life using that arm freely," Ophelia replied.

"I'm happy to meet for breakfast, but I don't know what else I can tell you about that night. I think, between the three of you, I've said it all," Ed said.

Before I had a chance to reply, the hostess returned, this time with Howard and Julia in tow. I recognized him from the security camera footage only, since he didn't have a picture attached to his LinkedIn profile. But this man was definitely Howard. He was on the shorter side, probably no more than five foot seven, carrying about fifty extra pounds around his middle. His brown hair was streaked with gray, and he didn't look like he brushed it very much. A couple of days of uneven stubble were on his face, but given what the man had just gone through, I couldn't really blame him if his personal hygiene wasn't front of mind at the moment.

His wife, Julia, on the other hand, looked like a celebrity who had just seen her husband die and was stoically facing the world. She was the same height as her husband, wearing a form-fitting light-blue tropical-print maxi dress and carrying a small designer clutch. Her spine was ramrod straight, and although she smiled at us, it didn't meet her eyes, which were the color of the ocean but had a haunted feel. The makeup she wore couldn't quite hide the bags under her eyes. This woman hadn't slept since the bomb went off, I could tell.

Was that because she was involved in setting it off? I wasn't sure yet.

I watched carefully as Howard took the seat next to Ed, and Julia sat on the other side of him. Was something really going on between them? Had

Howard specifically sat next to Ed to keep his wife from doing so? Or was it because the two were coworkers and he felt it was more polite?

"Thank you for meeting us," Ophelia said. "The three of us are working together to try and find who did this."

"We spoke to you the other day," Julia complained. "We've already told you everything we know. I don't understand why we have to go through this again."

"Because they have follow-up questions, and you don't know what could be useful," her husband replied quietly. Then, he turned to us. "Whatever you need. We'll answer."

"Did you notice at any point during the meal someone who didn't belong coming near your table?" I asked. "An employee, another customer, anyone?"

The three of them shook their heads in unison. "No. There really wasn't anyone. The table we were at, it was very private. There were palm trees that blocked us from the view of most people walking by, and it was near a corner ledge, so no one was going to walk past us by accident," Ed explained.

"Howard, you were facing the opposite direction from Julia and Ed," I said, flipping back in my notes to where I'd drawn out the setup of who was sitting where. "Is that right?"

"Yes. I was at the end of the table, facing south. I didn't see anyone, either, and they would have had to walk past me. Of course, it's possible they did. Just before the bomb went off, I was showing Courtney pictures of my daughter. It was really lucky, in fact. Courtney had moved over a chair to come to me. If she hadn't, she would have been closer to the explosion. I spoke to her last night."

"Did you?" Julia asked, her voice sharp.

Howard pressed his lips together. "I did. She's my boss. I wanted to see how she was doing. She's recovering well. She was very lucky. Though they've finally told her about Aiden. She was heartbroken."

"I don't understand why," Julia interrupted, shaking her head.

"You didn't like Aiden?" I asked.

"He was an idiot. Why a woman like Courtney married a man like that is completely beyond me. The man's head was so empty you could put helium through his ear and he'd float away."

"It's my understanding he was a pilot," I said.

Julia snorted. "That's what he wanted people to believe. He was a manager at a Barnes and Noble. I saw him there, a week before we left. And yet, he insisted people call him 'Captain,' and he spent half the flight talking everyone's ear off about the plane. *Did you know Airbus is a French company? I don't like them as much as Boeing myself. American engineering is always superior. Did you know Airbus call their winglets 'sharklets'? Oh, you wouldn't know what a winglet is. They're those little bits at the end of the wings that stick up. They look like they would make the plane slower, but they actually reduce drag, which makes the planes more efficient.*"

At the other end of the table, Ed let out a bit of a snort. "Yup, that was Aiden all right. *Did you know American Airlines has more A321s in their fleet than anyone else? It's insane to me that they don't buy Boeing planes, given their names, but that's the aviation business for you.*"

He looked across the table at Julia and flashed her a grin.

I was starting to think maybe Amir was right about the affair.

"You shouldn't speak ill of the dead, either of you," Howard said, shaking his head. "Aiden might not have been the easiest man to get along with, but he didn't deserve this. Courtney is so upset about his passing."

Julia rolled her eyes slightly, but it was enough that I could see it.

The server arrived then, and we each placed our orders. Ed and I both decided on the breakfast buffet and walked together toward the station.

"You have to forgive Julia," Ed told me. "She seems harsh, but she's grieving. She and Lara were really good friends."

"Lara died of a heart attack, didn't she?" I asked.

"Yes," Ed said quietly. "When she found out about Larry, her husband. She had never been in great health, and I guess it was all just too much for her to take. It's awful. She should have survived. She was in the bathroom with Julia when it happened."

"Are you having an affair with Julia?" I asked as Ed picked up a plate for the buffet. I watched closely for a reaction.

He stumbled, the plate falling back onto the pile with a clang. "Shit," he muttered then turned to me. "Sorry, what?"

"I think you heard what I asked, and I think you realize I already know the answer."

Ed closed his eyes. "How did you know?"

"Someone else in your group noticed. Then, I watched you and Julia this morning. I had a suspicion the other person in the group was right."

"You're not going to tell Howard, are you?" Ed asked, his eyes darting back in the direction of the table.

"So he doesn't know?"

"No. It's not… It's not really an affair, okay? It's just the two of us having a little bit of fun. Just on this trip. It wasn't more than that. I promise."

I nodded. "And you're sure Howard doesn't know?"

"Yeah. He's nice. I like him, but he's the kind of guy who just thinks about his work. That's why Julia and I got together. She wanted to enjoy Hawaii. Like, *enjoy* enjoy, if you know what I mean."

"I get it."

"Howard, on the other hand, treated this like a work trip. All he wanted to do was to get closer to

Courtney, professionally. He saw this week in Hawaii as a way to improve his relationship with his boss. His wife wanted more."

"Was it working?" I asked as Ed picked up another plate and moved over to the long table laden with delicious breakfast food. He used a pair of tongs to pick up a banana nut muffin, wincing slightly.

He shrugged as I grabbed a plate of my own. I slid farther down to a selection of fruit, grabbing a piece to make my plate look healthy, then continued on and piled a few slices of coconut French toast on my plate.

"Who knows?" he asked. "Honestly, I was here to have some fun, so I wasn't really paying attention. Larry kept trying to take over, as he always did, and so Howard was having to work hard just to get to Courtney."

"Larry was pretending he was in charge?"

"As always. That's what he did. He didn't like Courtney being the head of the team. He thought she was too young, and, to be honest, that she has a uterus didn't help. He thought he should have been in charge of the team. He would always do that. I think he figured if he could get everyone to see him as the boss, eventually Courtney's boss would have no choice but to replace her with him."

"Was there a chance of that happening?" I asked, my eyebrows rising.

"None," Ed said, spooning scrambled eggs onto

his plate. "Even if he succeeded, after what Courtney had just pulled off, she was going to be in charge of her own team for life. She's in charge of a group that just potentially made Valantir billions of dollars. She could rob a bank in broad daylight and go to jail for ten years and they still wouldn't demote her at this point. Larry just couldn't accept that Courtney was better at the job than he was."

"How long has the thing between you and Julia been going on?" I asked.

"Literally just started this trip. No longer. I think I've met her maybe twice in the past, total. At work functions."

"Are you going to keep seeing her after this trip ends?"

"Up to her," Ed replied, his eyes not meeting mine and instead focusing on the stack of sausages in the heated stainless-steel container. "I wouldn't say no if she's up for it. I like the lady. She's sexy. Older. I like that. But if she wants to go back to her normal life when we get back to the city, that's fine too."

"Who do you think did this, a few days later?" I asked. "Do you think it could have been someone in your group?"

Ed glanced down at the ground. "I don't know. I genuinely don't know. I've heard what Tom Kidd has to say about it. I know he's an idiot, but sometimes his guests are interesting. He's a controversial guy."

"You can say that again," I muttered.

"He says he was supposed to be the one there that night, at the table. If we're not looking at our competition, I have to think blowing up a dude who makes a living telling millions of people every week how using pronouns is ruining the country is more likely than blowing up a few scientists."

"The molecule you discovered—it can't have any harmful uses, right?"

"I mean, that's the thing about science. Anything can be used for good, or for evil. Potassium chloride has saved millions of lives by being used in heart medications, but if you inject too much of it into someone, they'll be dead within minutes. It's a molecule that could change the course of medicine as we know it. In a good way. But are there bad things that could be done with it as well? Almost certainly yes. We're not far enough into testing to know what those are, though."

"And the list of people who would know about it is small."

"Minuscule. Even if we were spied on by another company, everything is so hush-hush in this industry there wouldn't be more than five people who know about it. I guarantee you that. No one is out here trying to blow up scientists."

"Tom Kidd agrees, and is borderline suggesting that to people," I pointed out.

"Okay. You have a point. But I think he was the target. I think we're just a team of scientists and their family and friends who ended up in the wrong place at the wrong time. This has nothing to do with my affair with Julia. I'm telling you."

With that, Ed left the buffet area and walked back to the table, leaving me standing there with my half-full plate, thinking about what he'd just told me.

He was probably right. The timeline didn't make much sense. There was no opportunity for anyone to have dropped off a bomb with the scientist group.

Of course, it could have been Julia, or Lara, I realized with a start. They could have brought the bomb with them. They weren't at the table when it went off. They were in the bathroom. The others— there was no chance. The risks were too high. Why would they set off a bomb when they were likely to be its victims?

I filled up my plate and returned to the table. The topic of discussion had moved back to the bombing as well.

"Julia, you and Lara weren't at the table when it happened," Ophelia said. "What was the last thing you remember at the table before you left?"

The muscles around Julia's mouth tightened. "She saved my life, I think. Lara, I mean. She's the one who had to use the bathroom. She asked if I could come with her. I had a feeling she was getting frustrated with her husband and wanted a few minutes away."

"Frustrated?" I asked.

"He was a braggart," Julia explained. "It frustrated Lara. She was a shy woman and never wanted the limelight, but Larry was always painting himself as the leader of the group, and I know she found it embarrassing. Russell had just finished trying to tell Courtney something, but Larry kept interrupting them. She wanted to vent more than she wanted to use the bathroom."

"What did she tell you?" I asked.

"She said she wished Larry could understand that just because he tried to take over every meeting didn't mean he got to be in charge. She wanted him to be a bit more subtle. She said she knew he would be a good boss but that he felt like he had been set aside because of affirmative action. That Courtney only got the job because Valantir wanted to advertise that they had a certain number of women in leadership positions."

"Was that true?" Poppy asked.

Julia shrugged. "Wouldn't have a clue. I know I didn't warm to Larry. I'm not certain he would have been a good boss. He felt that being the loudest person in the room equated to being the most intelligent, and in my experience, the opposite is often the case."

I couldn't agree with Julia more.

"Lara was in the stall, and I stood by the sink. She was talking to me, and then we heard the sound. We had no idea what it was at first. I thought perhaps something had gone wrong in the kitchen.

But then we came out, and we saw everything, and oh. It was horrible. Lara ran forward, trying to find Larry, but there was too much going on. There was smoke and fire. I eventually grabbed her and told her we had to leave. We would find him later. I was sure of it. Little did I know. I didn't realize at the time that it was our table."

"Was anyone else in the bathroom with you at the time?" I asked.

"No. It was just the two of us."

I couldn't help but notice that meant Julia was by herself in the bathroom. If Lara was in one of the stalls, Julia could have pulled out a phone, dialled the number of the burner that would trigger the bomb, and set it off.

Mind you, that also meant Lara could have done it. But why would she set off a bomb and then die from the shock of learning her husband was dead? Wouldn't that have been the whole point? The bomb would have been right near where she was sitting. She would have had to have known he would be a likely target.

The conversation continued as we all ate, but we didn't learn anything new. As far as I was concerned, we had everything we were going to get from these victims. We'd spoken to Courtney and Amir already. If someone else who'd been at that table knew anything, they hadn't survived the blast.

As we left and headed back toward the room, I couldn't help but feel that Ed was right. We were probably heading in the wrong direction. It just straight-up didn't make sense logistically for any of the people at that table to have set off the bomb, and there seemed to be no other way for the bomb to have been planted.

That took us back to Tom Kidd either being the target, or having left it himself as one of the world's deadliest and stupidest publicity stunts.

Whether he was the intended victim, the perpetrator, or neither, he belonged in jail. It was time to go upstairs and make sure that was where he ended up.

Chapter 19

"What are you thinking?" Poppy asked Ophelia as we waited for an elevator to arrive. "Are you leaning toward anyone yet?"

"Yes," Ophelia said slowly. "I think I'm beginning to see what might have happened. However, I can't prove it yet, and I'm not sure how I'll be able to. I need to think about this. But we need to act fast."

"Who do you think it was?" I asked.

Ophelia shook her head. "Not until I know for certain. If I'm wrong, I don't want all six of us to look one way while the attacker gets away in the other."

The elevator arrived, and the doors opened with a *ding*. The three of us headed back up to the suite.

As soon as we entered, Taylor turned to us with a grin.

"When I get old, I want to be these ladies," she announced.

"What did I tell you about calling us old?" Dot replied, her gaze fixed on her screen.

"Right. I forgot. You were going to chop me up and turn me into fish food."

I laughed. "We've all been on the other end of that threat."

"Anyway, Dot knows what she's doing with this thing," Taylor said, motioning to the screen. "She might even be better at this than Fiona."

"Oh, I doubt that," Poppy said.

"I am better," Dot replied again, still not looking up. "Now, who wants to see a crime in progress? Because while the internet has been going insane, someone just broke into the home we've set up that belongs to Charlie's fake alter ego."

At that, the entire group immediately huddled around Dot's computers. The screens were much smaller than the ones she kept at home, but I could still make out what was going on.

The scene was the inside of a small apartment, a two-bedroom. It was neat and tidy, and I silently hoped that whatever was going to happen wouldn't involve completely trashing this place, because while I was totally willing to compensate Zoe's friend for whatever costs might be involved, I really didn't want him to have to return from his holiday to a destroyed apartment.

The entrance led to an open kitchen, a dining

room, and a living area. A small hallway led to the two bedrooms and the bathroom, which were both visible on other screens. One of the bedrooms was used as a home office, with a desk underneath the window and a small cabinet in the corner. I couldn't help but notice the small touches Dot had added to make it look like a young woman podcaster really lived there.

Recording equipment was all over the place. On the wall of the office was a large canvas emblazoned with the logo for my fake podcast, *At Becky's Call*. On the other wall was a promotional poster for the podcast, with one of the AI-generated photos of Becky that looked creepily like me staring back.

Dot had gone above and beyond in making this character believable.

At the front door, three men had just walked in. They pulled off the masks they wore to hide their faces, and I grinned. One was Tom Kidd himself, in the middle. The second I didn't recognize; he was around six feet tall, with a scraggly brown beard and beady eyes that darted around nervously. The third was the security guard I'd met at Tom's home.

"Right," said Tom. "We have to get something on this bitch. Calvin, we're looking for computers and files. See what we can find. Josh, you're looking around for anything physical that we can use. And all of you, make sure to use your gloves. Leave everything in place if you can. We don't want her to know we've been here. Her Instagram says she's at an event, but we want to be out of here within half an hour. You both get an extra fifty grand if we have something within that timeline. If we encounter anyone, I'll use my MMA skills to put them down."

I snorted at that.

"Yes, boss," the two others replied in unison, and I watched as the three men set about methodically trying to find something on Becky that would get her in trouble.

"This is like watching someone play a video game and seeing the points go up with every move they make, but the high score is actually jail time," Taylor said.

"I count four felonies off the top of my head," Rosie agreed. "There's no doubt about it; he's going to jail for a long time."

I watched with rapt attention as the three men split up and went through the apartment. It was immediately obvious this was not their first rodeo. They moved swiftly, with the confidence of men who had done this before. Within seconds, Tom and Calvin were in the bedroom that appeared to be an office, and Calvin sat down at the desk with the computer.

"I need something good for this bitch, Calvin. I mean it. We have to really destroy her life. She fucking embarrassed me. Hayley Yarrow. I can't believe it. She's next on my list. We'll have to see if we can hack her from here. She'll have security in person. Ugly, fat bitch."

"Focus, Tom," Calvin replied from his seat at the computer. "Right now, we're finding something on Becky. Ruin her reputation first, and Hayley's topples down with her. They're like dominos."

"Fat dominos," Kidd muttered sulkily under his breath.

"I'm truly shocked that a man like that isn't married," Poppy said, rolling her eyes.

"What's scarier is the number of men who agree with him," Taylor said. "If he was really so repulsive to everyone, he wouldn't have a platform."

"That is exactly right," Ophelia replied, her eyes not moving from the screen. "Dot, there's no chance that they're going to find the cameras you've put in place, is there?"

"What do you think I am, some sort of amateur?"

"Fair enough."

"This is state-of-the art equipment. I'm not playing," Dot said. "They didn't bring them, but they could have had scanners designed to find hidden cameras, and those wouldn't have registered these."

"If you tell me you broke into an NSA site and stole their prototypes, I'm going to be very impressed," Taylor said. "And also I'd like to come along on your next field trip."

That response caused Dot to crack a smile. "Not quite. I have my sources. But you don't need to worry. Not only is everything Kidd is doing on camera right now, but he's not going to know about it until the police break down his door."

"What's happening, Calvin? Why is this taking so long?" Tom asked, and my attention turned back to the video screen. Tom was pacing back and forth behind Calvin, who was squinting at the computer screen.

Josh, the security guard, was rifling through the items in the closet in the other bedroom.

"I don't know, man," Calvin said. "It's weird. There's, like, extra security on this thing. I can't get in the way I normally do."

"Well, do something else. We have to get into this computer."

"I'm trying. Look, why don't you start going through that cabinet? Then we can save some time. Maybe you'll find something there."

Tom nodded, but he was obviously upset. "I don't pay you to fail at this. It's a computer. You've done this a million times for me. How hard can it be?"

"Don't worry. I'll get there. I've never met a computer I couldn't crack."

Dot grinned. "There's a first time for everything, honey."

Tom began going through the files in the cabinet.

"There's nothing particularly good in there," Dot said. "I don't want him to find what he's after in this home. He has to steal the computer."

Minutes passed, and Tom was obviously becoming more and more agitated.

"Why aren't you in yet?" he asked Calvin then grabbed a stack of papers and threw them on the ground.

"I don't know, man. I'm doing my best, okay? I know you're stressed, but we have to leave everything the way it was."

."Fuck it. We have to get out of here. We have nothing. Everything good she's going to have is on that computer. We need to get in."

Calvin frowned. "I can't. There's some sort of extra security here. I can't break through the way I normally do."

"Then break into it some other way," Tom snapped. "I don't have all day. We need to go."

Josh chose that moment to join the others in the second bedroom. "Sorry, boss. Nothing good out there. As far as anyone knows, she's squeaky clean. Got nothing more than a really freaky vibrator in the bedroom."

"I borrowed that from Vesper," Dot said with a grin. "Dildo Daggins."

I groaned. "And here I was hoping I'd never have to hear that name again."

"Fantastic," Taylor said, laughing. "Mine's Buzzy. To infinity and beyond."

I groaned. "Can we not talk about what you named your dildos, please?"

"You're such a prude," Dot shot back at me.

Before I could respond, the conversation on the screen resumed.

"I need some of the tools I have back home to get into this," Calvin said.

"You know the rules. We don't leave a trace that we were here," Josh told him.

The two men looked at Tom, their boss, for direction.

"You're sure there's no way you're going to break into this? What did she get, some nerd to help her?"

"She must have. An extra layer of security most people don't bother with. I can get in—I'm sure I can—but I need more time, and I need some more sophisticated equipment."

"You couldn't have brought it with you just in case?" Tom asked, kicking at the air in a way that was reminiscent of five-year-olds throwing a tantrum.

"No. It's too much. I can't just carry it around with me. Especially when we're not supposed to be drawing attention to ourselves."

"Okay, fine," Tom said. He pinched the bridge between his nose then made his decision. "We take it with us. But we can't keep it at my place. Or yours, Calvin. Becky will know we were here, and we'll be the first people the cops call. I'll get a friend to give us an alibi, but we have to make sure no one knows where this computer is."

"I'll leave it at my brother's place," Calvin said.

"I won't tell him about it. He has a storage unit that I have access to. I'll take my stuff there and do the work in it, then I'll destroy it."

"Good," Tom said. "We'll do that."

"The fly has flown directly into our web," Ophelia said with a smile.

Calvin leaned down, grabbed the desktop computer's power cord, and unplugged it. He then grabbed the computer's frame and unplugged the cords connecting it to the monitor and keyboard. The three of them rushed back out of the apartment.

"And scene," Dot said with a flourish. "I've got all of this recorded. I'll track down the address for Calvin's brother's computer, and you can give that to Jake along with the rest of this. He'll be grateful for the slam-dunk case."

"I'm going to insist that I be there when they arrest him," I said with a smile of my own. "I want him to know that it's a group of women who took him down."

"Not to mention his own hubris," Ophelia said. "Instead of immediately focusing on revenge, he should have been thinking about his own PR."

"He'll have at least ten years to think about it," Rosie replied.

"The only disappointing part is that he didn't admit to the bomb on the footage," I said. "In fact, he didn't mention it at all. I know that's now what we were going for, but it would have been a nice bonus if that had worked out."

"It almost would have been too convenient," Poppy said with a chuckle. "Like the sort of thing you read about in a book, or see in a movie."

"I guess so," I admitted. "Still, if that was a shortcut the universe was willing to give me, I would take it."

"I don't think this is where you're going to find the killer," Ophelia mused. "But we will find the proof we need to catch the bomber."

"It would help us if you told us what you were thinking," I pointed out, but Ophelia shook her head.

"No. I am not certain that I am right. I only have the slimmest of threads forming. Like a hen who has laid an egg but still needs to incubate it so it can hatch."

"Ophelia loves her animal metaphors, especially when she gets closer to the end of a case," Poppy explained.

"I think it's smart to keep each other informed but at arm's length," Rosie said. "You don't want to become the blind leading the blind."

"All right, I have to head home," Dot said. "It'll be easier to format everything and then send it to Charlie to give to Jake. We want to get this done as soon as possible, I assume?"

"That would be great," I said.

"In that case, we will leave you to it," Ophelia said. "Let us know how it goes."

"Record the arrest, if you can. I want to see the look on that fucker's face," Taylor chimed in.

"I'll do my best," I replied.

Dot packed up her things. She, Rosie, and I left the hotel room.

"That went about as well as we could have hoped," Dot said in the elevator on the way down.

"I agree. The man deserves all the jail time he gets," Rosie added.

"Between waking up to find out he got roasted by one of the most famous people on social media and becoming the laughingstock of the country, to being arrested later today, I think this probably tops the list of bad days in Tom Kidd's life," I said, cackling. "That was fun. There's nothing I like more about this job than seeing bad people get what they deserve."

"That's half the cases," Rosie said. "Now we just need to find out who set off that bomb."

"I wonder," I said, half to myself. "I think we've got most of the data we're going to get. Now I just have to sort through this information to figure it out."

"Ophelia seems to have an idea," Dot said.

"She does. She won't share it until she has proof, though. I don't care if she's the one who figures it out. I have an ego but not when it comes to finding killers."

"Good," Rosie said.

Dot drove her own car home, and I gave Rosie a ride to her place then headed back to my own, thinking about what I'd learned this morning about the Valantir employees and the bomb. How had it gotten there? Who was it left for?

I had a feeling the answer to both questions was Tom Kidd.

But I still had to prove it.

Chapter 20

Zoe pulled into her parking spot next to mine just as I was getting out of my car. It was now just before noon.

"Hey, how was your shift?" I asked.

"Not too bad. The middle of the night and the early morning are usually fairly tame. Unless it's a Friday or Saturday. Then you get a few more people who have overdone it at the bars. But that wasn't the case last night. It was quiet enough, by ER standards. How about you?"

"I guess you haven't seen the news. Tom Kidd just got roasted like a Kahlua pig before a big event, and he decided to take his revenge out on my alter ego, who doesn't really exist. As soon as I get the proof of it to Jake and he can get a warrant, he's going to jail."

Zoe chuckled. "Glad to know I've got that to look forward to upstairs. What are you up to?"

"I'm waiting for Dot to send me the files so I can forward them on to Jake and trying to solve my bombing case. I still haven't gotten to the bottom of it."

"Have you spoken to your mom yet?"

"No."

"Are you planning on avoiding her for the rest of your life so you never have to have a real, adult conversation with her about the fact that she's dating someone again?"

"Yes."

"At least you're recognizing it."

"I'll talk to her. Eventually. Just not now. Plus, I'm not going to call her up and be like, 'Oh, hi, Mom. By the way, I saw you bringing a man home last night.' I can't do that."

"Fair enough. She'll tell you when she's comfortable too. She probably wants to protect you. She knows how much you loved your dad."

"I know," I said with a sigh. "Funnily enough, that part doesn't really bug me. I know Dad would want Mom to be happy, including if that meant finding someone else. It's just… It's weird."

"It's a change, for sure," Zoe agreed. "But change isn't always bad. He might be a nice guy."

"If he hurts her, I'm turning him into fish food."

Zoe laughed. "I wouldn't expect anything less."

The two of us walked toward the entrance, and I asked, "How are things going with Henry?"

Zoe's face lit up. "Really great, actually. Yeah,

it's good. He understands my job better than anyone I've ever met. There's no whining about the fact that I'm doing triple shifts, or working in the middle of the night. He has his own life, and he doesn't try to control mine."

"That's great."

"And when our schedules do match up and we can spend time together, it's awesome. He loves the water as much as I do."

I crinkled up my face. "He sounds perfect for you."

Zoe laughed. "It might be a bit early to say that, but yeah, right now I'm happy. Things are good. I'm really glad you introduced us."

"I call dibs on being maid of honor at your wedding."

Zoe rolled her eyes. "We're very far from having *that* conversation, but whoever I marry, you're obviously going to be my maid of honor."

"My speech will involve me telling the story of the murder case that brought you two together."

"Maybe not the most appropriate venue for that story."

"It's fine. I'll make it funny."

Zoe cocked an eyebrow in my direction as we entered the apartment. "Only you could think to make a murder funny. I'm going to hop in the shower."

I settled in on the couch with Coco, who was fast asleep, and pulled out a notepad. I wanted to scribble down what I knew. Sometimes just writing everything down, seeing the facts in a different format, made me think of the facts of the case differently and led to breakthroughs.

Before I began to write, though, I called Jake.

"Hey," he said to me when he answered. "What's up?"

"You owe me. Dinner at MonkeyPod? You're buying. And I'm getting all the fancy cocktails on their menu, because our plan worked."

"I'm listening," Jake said.

"We have video footage of Tom Kidd and two accomplices breaking into an apartment and stealing a computer. We're running down the storage unit where it's being kept—it belongs to the brother of one of the thieves."

"And this was you and those investigators from San Francisco?"

"Sure was."

"You know, I thought you and those two old ladies who always seem to be suspiciously involved in your schemes were the only three people crazy enough to do things like this. Apparently, I was wrong."

"I've found my people," I replied.

"It sure looks like it."

"You're not at my feet, bowing down to me, as much as you should be right now, by the way. I'm giving you Tom Kidd on a platter."

Jake laughed. "I thought I was waiting for

MonkeyPod. Unlimited cocktails, on me. Can you send the footage over?"

"Will do, as soon as I have it. Also, I have one more condition."

"Uh-oh."

"I want to be there when he's arrested. I want him to know it was me."

"Okay, Olenna Tyrell."

"Hey, she was a boss."

"She was," Jake agreed.

"Great, so I'm coming."

"There are conditions," Jake replied. "But I think we can make this happen, especially since I know that if I don't, you'll just refuse to send me the files."

"You know me so well," I sang.

"But I mean it. There are procedures to follow when arresting someone, and it's dangerous. He's dangerous. We both know he's committed crimes, but we don't know how many."

"He might have been the one who set the bomb off at the resort the other day," I pointed out. "I know what I'm getting into."

"Okay. Look, it should be fine. You can come. But you're not allowed to talk. You're an observer. Nothing else. Understood?"

"What if I have a pithy saying to throw out there?"

I could practically feel Jake closing his eyes and

taking a breath on the other end of the line. "No pithy sayings."

"Fine."

"Send me the video, and I'll run it past my captain and get a warrant from a judge. It shouldn't take long. I'll be in touch."

"Will do. And Jake?"

"Yeah?"

"Thanks for agreeing. I know this is hard for you."

"You're welcome. It's not hard, I want to see the look on his face too."

I ended the call, grinning away like an idiot. This day was already good, and it was going to become an even better one.

I FORWARDED THE VIDEOS DOT HAD SENT ME THEN spent about forty-five minutes mulling over all the facts I had gathered on the bombing up until that point. I chatted it out a bit with Zoe as she made some food after her shower. After that, I took Coco out to do her business and even asked her if she had any ideas.

Unfortunately, even Coco came up empty, and by the time Jake called me back, I was no closer to an answer. I was missing something. I was sure of it. We had all the facts. There had to be something here, something that would be the key to solving this case.

I just didn't know what it was.

When Jake asked if I was ready to go, I was bursting at the seams with nervous energy. I dressed back up in my Becky Byrd outfit, said goodbye to Zoe, who was already wearing her bonnet and robe and going through her bedtime routine, then gave Coco some food and headed out.

I wasn't going to miss this for the world.

"We're getting ready to go. I'll have Liam with me, so I'll meet you at the parking lot before the turnoff," Jake said.

"Sounds good. I don't want to ride with Liam anyway. I can feel myself getting dumber by the second when I spend time with him."

"And Charlie?"

"Yeah?"

"If anything starts to go wrong, I want you to get out of there. Promise me that. You can't get hurt, okay? I can't handle it if you get hurt."

"I promise."

I ended the call and began the drive back up to Tom Kidd's home. It was a gorgeous late winter afternoon on Maui. The sun was shining, a few puffy white clouds dotted the sky without blocking its rays, and I let my skin soak in the vitamin D as the wind whipped my hair. This was one of the best times of year to be on the island. The weather was perfect.

An absolutely stunning day to ruin the life of a man who deserved it.

I parked Queenie in the tiny lot on the shoulder of the highway, next to the path that led down to Honolua Bay—one of Maui's worst beaches and best spots for snorkeling and surfing, depending on the weather. It was one of Zoe's favorite places, year-round—in the winter she surfed, and in the summer she snorkeled and hung out with the *honu* that made the bay their home—but if I was going to the beach, I wanted to lie on the white sand, not have rocks the size of baseballs digging into my back.

About three minutes later, a police cruiser came past, and I flagged down Jake and Liam. Once I climbed into the back seat, we continued the short drive to Tom Kidd's place.

"For the record, I didn't want you coming," Liam said, glancing at me through the side mirror.

"It's okay. I know you've never made anybody come," I shot back.

"Charlie," Jake said, warning in his voice.

"This is why I can't stand you," Liam said. "You're mean. You didn't have to say that."

"You started it. I literally wouldn't have said anything to you if you hadn't been a dick first."

"Yeah, but yours was *mean*."

"Only because I'm smart enough to come up with a better insult than 'I don't like you.'"

"It's a whole two minutes," Jake muttered under

his breath. "You couldn't make it through a two-minute drive."

He turned off toward Kidd's home, and before I knew it, we were at the gate.

"Maui Police," Jake said, holding his badge up to the camera. "We're here to speak to Tom Kidd."

No one replied, but the gate opened, letting us through. They probably thought Jake was just here to ask more questions about the bombing.

Jake pulled up to the expansive house and got out of the car, with Liam following. I was just getting out of the passenger-side door when I heard Tom's voice.

"Look, I know you're here because you have questions about the bomb, but it's really not a good time. I have a lot happening today, and I appreciate that you have a job to do, but if we could make this quick, I would really appreciate it."

I grinned, slipping out of the car without showing myself. Because I was on the far side of the car, it wouldn't be immediately obvious to Tom that I was there.

"All right," Jake said. To anyone else, he would have sounded like a consummate professional, but I knew him well enough to hear the undertone of amusement in his voice. He was going to enjoy this as much as I did.

Okay, maybe not *as* much. But it would be close.

"Tom Kidd, you're under arrest," Jake continued. "You have the right to remain silent. Anything you say can and will be used against you in a court of law."

"What? Arrested? What the hell for?" Tom boomed. "Don't you know who I am?"

"You have the right to an attorney," Jake continued. "If you cannot afford one, one will be provided for you."

He stepped toward Tom, who backed away, holding his hands up in front of him. "Hold on. There's a mistake. There's got to be. What am I being arrested for?"

"Breaking and entering, and theft," Jake replied.

"Theft? Breaking and entering? What the… how… no! No, this isn't happening. Who's responsible for this?"

This was my cue. I popped up and came around the front of the car, arms wide, like I was Russel Crowe in *Gladiator*, celebrating after a massive win. "Surprise, bitch!"

Liam glared at me while Tom stood frozen in place, his mouth dropping open. His eyes widened as the realization came to him that he was, well and truly, completely screwed.

"You," he finally spluttered. "What did you do?"

"Oh, I know you'd love to blame this on women, but it's all your own actions sending you to jail, baby," I said while Jake reached his arms behind him and placed handcuffs on the man. Liam was off to the side, putting cuffs on Cody, the security guard.

"This is bullshit," Tom spat in my direction. "You bitch. How dare you? You're trying to ruin my life. You know what, Becky? I'm going to destroy you. I'm going to make you wish you were never born. I have more money than God. And I didn't do shit, so when I get out of jail, I'm going to hunt you down and make you regret you were ever born."

I held a hand up to my mouth and yawned. "Boring. You're boring. For one thing, far scarier men than you have threatened me before. Like oh no, what am I afraid of? The guy who ran away to his panic room when he thought there was an intruder in his house? Yeah, truly, you're terrifying. Where were those MMA moves you keep talking about? Second, you're not getting out of jail. Not for a long time. Believe me. I'm not scared of you. I'm laughing at you."

"All right, let's go," Jake said, shoving Tom roughly toward the police cruiser.

"You can't do this," Tom said, his voice rising in pitch. "You can't arrest me. I'm Tom Kidd! I can't go to jail. I'll get you fired for this. It's all going on my show. The Maui PD is corrupt. They're arresting me for something I didn't do. They're trying to silence me! This isn't going to work."

"Sorry, honey, I think your show's just gone off the air for good," I said, flipping Tom Kidd off as Jake pushed his head down and forced him into the cruiser.

Tom let out a loud howl, like a wounded animal,

as Liam shoved Cody in after him. The security guard, for his part, was handling his arrest much more professionally. He didn't resist, just calmly entered the car, while Tom was still screaming about the injustice of it all.

As Liam slammed the door shut behind them, Tom's screaming turned into nothing more than dull background noise.

Jake strode toward me. "What did I say about not talking?" he asked.

"I know, but I couldn't resist. I'm a dramatic person."

"No kidding."

"Plus, you have to admit, this was way more fun. The look on his face was so worth it."

Jake cracked a smile. "Okay. Fine. I'll admit it, that was a hell of a meltdown. And I can turn the threats into more charges."

"That's what I like to hear."

"I've got to go. I'll see you later, okay? We're going to drop these guys off in holding and get them processed, and then I've got to follow up another lead on that burglary case."

"Cool, I can make my own way back to my car. The entertainment on the way back is bound to be loud."

Jake rolled his eyes. "I really wish they'd make these cars soundproof sometimes. See you later, Charlie."

"Bye."

I watched as the police cruiser headed off toward the front gate and exited the home. I followed on foot after the car, unable to help grinning to myself.

Tom Kidd's reign of stupidity was over.

Chapter 21

I TOOK MY TIME WALKING BACK TO QUEENIE, enjoying the fresh air and the warmth of the day, before climbing in and putting some music on as I drove toward Kihei.

The others would have been watching live footage of Tom getting arrested—it was the same camera as I'd used in his home, which used Bluetooth to record to my phone and share the saved footage with Dot—and I couldn't wait for us all to celebrate together.

Was there more to this, though? Would interrogation get Tom to admit he had also set the bomb off? After all, making himself out as the supposed victim was the perfect way to drive suspicion away from himself.

Suddenly, I gasped. Everything clicked. I slammed on the brakes and pulled Queenie over to the side of the road while I ran through it all. It made perfect sense. Every part of it. And I knew exactly why I hadn't thought of it before.

I knew who had set off the bomb.

I pulled back out onto the road, speeding toward Kahului as fast as I could. I needed to be sure. My heart raced in my chest. The more I thought about it, the more I knew I was right. I had to be. Now I just had to prove it.

Pulling into the hospital, I changed from Becky back to Charlie and walked to the front counter and asked the nurse if I could go in and speak with Courtney. She was the key to all of this.

She was the bomber.

I was led into her room, where she was propped up on the bed, looking significantly better than she had a few days ago. The color had returned to her cheeks, the bandage on the side of her head was smaller, and she smiled at me as I entered.

"Charlie, was it? It's nice to see you again. Have you gotten any closer to finding the person who set the bomb off?"

"I think so," I said.

Courtney's eyes watched me as I walked in, taking my time.

I wanted her to be nervous. I wanted her to wonder what I was going to say next so that when I did, it hit with all of the emotional impact of, well, a bomb. "It was you."

I watched Courtney's reaction carefully. She sat stock-still, blinking slowly, before responding a few seconds later. If she was surprised, she didn't show it.

She smiled slightly. "Now, there's a joke if I've ever heard one. Hilarious."

"I'm not joking. I know it was you."

Courtney motioned around. "Are you serious? Look at where I am. I'm in the hospital. I had surgery. I nearly died. My husband is dead."

"That was the point, wasn't it? To kill Aiden. And if Larry went, too, since he was across the table from him, well, that was just a nice added bonus, right?"

"What in the world are you talking about?" Courtney asked. "You're insane. I'm calling a nurse."

"Go ahead. But then you'll never know what I know. What I've figured out. And how I'm going to throw you in jail for it."

Courtney paused, considering, then narrowed her eyes at me and leaned back in the bed. "All right. Fine. You can tell me your ridiculous story, and then I'll tell you how it's wrong, and you can go find the actual killer."

"Sure. Let's do that. I don't know if you *planned* on murdering your husband before coming to the island, but you went through with it the other day. Maybe it was how he was constantly pretending to be a pilot, when really he was just a manager at Barnes and Noble. Or maybe it was how he constantly put you down in front of your employees when you had worked tooth and nail to get where you were, while morons like Larry fought you every step of the way because they were offended having a penis and skin the color of corn starch wasn't enough by itself to get them a promotion."

Courtney rolled her eyes. "It was constant. A nonstop barrage. He was always trying to butt in, to pretend he was the head of the team, when in reality, he was a middling biologist with zero management skills. There's a reason I was promoted and he wasn't. But that doesn't mean he deserved to die."

"Doesn't it? I think you believed it did. Now, you can correct me if I'm wrong, but here's how I think things happened: it all started on the plane. Aiden was pretending to all your coworkers that he was a pilot, annoying them with facts about the plane that anyone could have looked up with a simple Google search. Then, not only that, but he would put you down in front of them, to make himself look smarter. It started getting to you. Somewhere along the line, you read about the movement to limit or stop tourism to Hawaii, and you saw an opportunity."

"None of this is true," Courtney interrupted, but I continued.

"You're a manager, but you're also a scientist. You know how chemistry and physics work. You knew how to make an easy explosive with a few ingredients you could buy at the pharmacy. Because you're intelligent, you probably hit up a few different ones. Maybe on other sides of the island. You paid cash. But this is a small island, Courtney. It's not going to take long before I hunt down the security footage from all the pharmacies on the island. And when I do, I'm going to find you on it, aren't I? Buying the ingredients needed to make TATP."

This time, Courtney didn't respond. Her gaze was fixed on me.

"So, you decided enough was enough. You'd had it with your husband. You built a bomb. Knowing what you do about science, it wasn't hard, I'm sure. And you'd know exactly how much of every chemical you'd need to build something that could hurt you but would kill your husband. Let me ask you, was Larry just a bonus? Or had you planned on killing him from the start too?"

"I didn't do this," Courtney repeated, but her voice lacked the conviction it held before. I was close.

I shrugged. "You built this bomb, knowing that you would be a victim. But you set it up so you wouldn't be killed, just injured. Not only could you try and pin the bombing on people trying to attack tourism on the island, but you were giving yourself some extra insurance: no one would ever expect someone to bomb a table they were sitting at. That'd be insane, right?"

"It is insane."

"For a regular person, sure. But you knew what

you were doing. You weren't some amateur making a pipe bomb in their basement. You're a scientist. You built a bomb, and on that last night, you took it to dinner. You sat in the middle of the table, knowing that Larry would have taken a seat on one side of you, didn't you? After all, he was always trying to undermine you. Aiden sat across from him, and then you waited. Until the perfect moment."

I paused and looked at her. "Howard wanted you to look at pictures, so you moved from your seat, to the left, and I'm going to guess you probably also turned the chair away from the rest of the table under the guise of seeing better, but it was actually to protect you from the blast. Lara, Larry's wife, had gone to the bathroom along with Julia, so she wouldn't be hit by the blast. Larry, Aiden, Amir, and Russel were the main people in the line of fire. And so, you took the chance and set off the bomb. But there was a worker there too. Emily. She died, and she didn't deserve it. Did you know she was there? She was trying to make enough money to go to college."

Courtney gave me a hard look. "No. I didn't know."

"So you admit it."

Courtney shrugged. "I guess there's no point in avoiding it at this point, is there? You've obviously figured it all out. You're right. I did set the bomb. I brought it with me in my tote bag. No one had a clue. I slid it under the table and kicked it toward

Aiden just before I moved chairs to look at Larry's phone. I wanted to come out of it injured but not dead. No one would suspect me. I never let on how much Aiden frustrated me. How much Larry annoyed me. At work and at home, I was constantly undermined. Do you know what that's like? To always have a man, every single second of your life, trying to make you feel like you're not worthy?"

"Divorce lawyers do exist for precisely this reason," I pointed out.

"I make so much more money than Aiden. This was much cheaper. And as a bonus, I got Larry too. I do feel bad about that poor server. I didn't realize she was at the other end of the table when the bomb went off. I never meant for her to get hurt. And Lara—I thought she would have been safe, being in the bathroom. But her heart was too weak."

"And Russel?"

"It's sad, but it had to happen. Collateral damage. It happens in war, and that's what this was. A war."

I nodded. "Well, thanks for admitting it to me. Are you going to turn yourself in, or do you need me to find the evidence the hard way?"

"Oh," Courtney said. "I don't think you need to worry about that at all."

And with that, she leapt out of the bed and ran toward me, a syringe held in her hand like a knife.

I didn't know what was in that syringe, but I had

a sneaking suspicion it wasn't great. Instinctively, I darted to the right and out of Courtney's way, kicking out as I went past her.

She fell to the floor with a cry but then reached out and grabbed my ankle.

I felt a stabbing pain in my leg, and I screamed as I saw the syringe sticking out of my lower calf. I kicked out and hit Courtney in the face with my other leg.

The move stunned her enough that she let go of my ankle.

I slid out from her grasp and scooched along the floor on my arms and legs to get away from her. My back hit a nursing cart, and I reached up to the top of it, desperate to grab something, anything, to use as a weapon.

My fingers closed around a box, and I grabbed it, hurling it toward Courtney. Unfortunately, it was full of large Band-Aids. Not exactly the most effective weapon available.

Upon scrambling to my feet with the help of the cart, I grabbed a small metal bowl and swung it as hard as I could at Courtney as she got up and prepared to take me on once more.

My swing connected harder than Mike Trout hitting a homer, and a clang rang out through the room before Courtney collapsed to the floor, unconscious.

I paused, breathing heavily, looking down at her before my gaze fell to the syringe sticking out of my leg. Oh no. Oh no, oh no, oh no. The plunger hadn't been pressed, but oh, this was bad.

I rushed out into the hall. "Zoe?" I called out instinctively, my head spinning around as I looked for my best friend.

A nurse emerged from a nearby room and immediately registered something was wrong. "What's happening?" she asked me.

"Security. I need security. I was attacked by a patient. And this," I said, motioning to my leg.

The nurse immediately jumped into action. "Okay. Take a deep breath. Stand here. I'm calling security."

The nurse grabbed a phone on the wall and muttered something into it. Then she returned and looked at my leg. "Security are on their way. I'm going to remove the syringe, okay?"

I nodded, my head still spinning. I closed my eyes while the nurse yanked the syringe out, and I breathed a sigh of relief. I'd never been great with needles at the best of times, let alone when they'd just been thrust into my leg like this.

"What was it?" I asked.

The nurse had a look at the side. "A sedative. Who did this to you?"

"Courtney Silva," I replied. "I confronted her as she's the bomber, and she stabbed me with this."

The nurse gasped. "Really? Courtney? She's the one who killed all those people?"

I nodded. "Yup. How long would it have taken

for this to take effect if she'd pressed in the plunger?"

"Twenty seconds or so and you would have been unconscious."

Bile rose in my throat. No doubt, Courtney would have planned to knock me out and then kill me. What she would have done with my body was beyond me, but she probably hadn't thought that far ahead, either. If she'd managed to inject me with the sedative, though, there was no doubt that I'd have been dead.

At that moment, security arrived, and I quickly explained the situation to them.

They entered the room to find Courtney still unconscious on the floor.

It was over. The bomb maker had been found.

And the camera hidden in my necklace would have recorded every second of what had just happened, as it had Tom Kidd's arrest. Courtney was going to jail for the rest of her life.

Chapter 22

I WAITED AT THE HOSPITAL FOR THE POLICE TO arrive.

Courtney was taken out in handcuffs. While she waited, she'd been taken to the security offices where she came to about ten minutes later. She hadn't said a word since. The only thing she said when she saw the police arrive was, "I demand to speak with an attorney."

It didn't matter. No lawyer would be able to get her off from this case. As soon as the video came out showing her admitting to the crime, it was over. The police would visit local pharmacies. They all had security cameras set up, and they would get the backups and find Courtney buying the ingredients to make the bomb.

There was no way she was getting out of this. Not to mention, she was also facing assault charges for what had happened to me.

Once I'd given my statement to the police, I left the hospital—it turned out Zoe's shift wasn't starting for another half hour, so she wasn't there anyway—and hopped into Queenie. I put the phone on speaker and dialled Dot's number before driving off.

"I didn't know they were having a two-for-one sale on sending terrible people to jail," Dot said as she answered. "Good job, Charlie."

"Thanks. I was hoping you'd see the show on the camera feed. Where are you?"

"At the hotel, with the others. Come on down. We're going to celebrate. And I know Ophelia has a hundred questions to ask you. She's impressed that you figured out it was Courtney. We all are."

"Thanks," I said, warmth rising inside me. "It clicked as I was leaving after Tom Kidd's arrest. I'm heading down there now. I'll see you soon."

I ended the call, put my phone away, and started Queenie. Leaving the hospital, I let the successes of the day wash over me. Tom Kidd was going to jail for breaking into a home to steal secrets because someone made fun of him on the internet. Courtney had admitted to building and setting off the bomb, injuring herself in the process, just to kill her husband and co-worker who annoyed her, because she didn't want to pay alimony in a divorce.

We had done it.

I reached the Maui Diamond resort and parked the car. The first thing I did was leave a message for

Marina, letting her know that we'd found the bomber and that she was in police custody.

Then, I went up to the suite, where Poppy answered the door. As soon as I entered, cheers rang out.

"There she is!" Taylor shouted. "The woman of the hour. Come over here and get sloshed. You deserve it."

I laughed as I made my way into the room.

Taylor was in the suite's kitchenette, lifting a bottle of champagne the size of a large toddler into the air. She poured me a flute and slid it across the table.

I grabbed it and happily held it up high. "To all of us. Everything that happened today was thanks to our teamwork. Who knew there was a group of women just as crazy as we are out on the mainland?"

"Hear, hear," Poppy agreed, and cheers rose once more.

I took a sip of champagne and made my way toward Dot, who had a flute of her own sitting next to the computer.

Rosie held one in her hand next to her, but I couldn't help but notice it wasn't touched.

"Not much of a drinker?" I asked, my eyes flitting down to her glass.

"For obvious reasons, I never allow my senses to be dulled by anything if I can help it, nor my inhibitions," she replied. "All the same, it's best to pretend to partake. Good work today."

"Thanks. I got lucky. I realized as I was leaving what I'd missed. It was assuming that the victims couldn't have set the bomb."

"It was the perfect alibi," Dot agreed, nodding. "No one ever thinks a victim of a crime is also the one committing it."

"It was Ophelia who came up with the idea first," I said, motioning to her as she came over. "She mentioned maybe it was Tom Kidd who had planted it then set it off after his group had left. The idea was that the perpetrator was meant to be the victim. That was what planted the seed in my mind, I guess. But something else wasn't fitting. I couldn't get all the puzzle pieces to slot in, until I thought about it: what if one of the victims *at* the table was the one who set off the bomb? And then it clicked. Everything made sense. Courtney had moved away from where she'd left the bomb. The two men giving her the most grief in her life were two of the victims. She had the knowledge to not only build a bomb but to make one that would injure her but not kill her."

"That's still so risky," Poppy said, shaking her head. "All that, just to get away from her husband? It could have gone wrong so easily."

"It could have," Ophelia said. "I think there was more to it than wanting a divorce. She wanted to kill him. I think for her to have hated him so much she was willing to kill him, after over a decade of marriage, this was about more than the money."

"I agree," I chimed in. "This was more than pragmatics. But the way she did it, to make herself a victim, too, and kill so many completely innocent people along the way? It shows how awful she is. She would have killed me, too, if she could have."

"I'm glad you're okay," Poppy said.

"Don't worry. It'll take more than just one murderous psychopath to get rid of Charlie here," Dot said, shooting me a wink.

Ophelia turned toward her and Rosie. "It was lovely to meet the two of you as well. You're very interesting. Although there is something I can't quite put my finger on happening with you, Rosie."

Rosie gave Ophelia a polite smile. "Whatever could you mean? I'm just an ordinary retiree."

Ophelia's face cracked into a curious expression. "That's the thing. I don't believe you are. You're hiding something, and I can't quite tell what. That you're doing it successfully means you're very, very good at it."

"She means that," Taylor interrupted. "I once saw Ophelia catch a war criminal within twenty minutes of landing in Sydney. He'd undergone more plastic surgery than my aunt Rita after she decided she wanted to look like Lucille Ball. But he walked past Ophelia while we were waiting in line for coffee, and thirty seconds later, she was on the phone with Interpol."

Ophelia shrugged. "I knew from others' testimony that he had a habit of rubbing the thumb and ring finger of his left hand together when he was thinking. Besides, most people who change their appearance never put the effort in to change their gait. The gait will always give you away. But you, Rosie. Nothing gives you away."

"Maybe that's because I have nothing to hide," Rosie said, shooting her a wink.

"Oh no, that's not it. But I respect that you are one of the first people I have ever come across whose secrets I cannot uncover. Whatever you are hiding, you do it very well. Your secret is safe. I know you well enough to believe you are a good person, and I consider you a friend. A friend that I respect very much."

"And I can say the same about you," Rosie replied. The two women shared a look that obviously said a lot more than the words they shared. They were really alike in a lot of ways, and they understood that.

"If you're ever in San Francisco, come say hi," Poppy said. "I'd love to show you around our city. And maybe have you help out with a case or two. This was fun."

"It was," Ophelia agreed. "And I don't work very well with other people."

"She's not lying. Half the San Francisco PD secretly wants her to fail," Poppy added with a smile.

"If I did, they'd have half the solve rate they currently do for violent crime."

"Yeah, well, I never said they were smart."

I laughed, and my phone rang. It was Mom. "Hold on, I have to take this, I'll be right back." I stepped out of the room and into the hallway, where I tapped the green button to answer the call.

"Charlie?"

"Hi, Mom. What's up?"

Through the phone, I could hear her taking a deep breath. "I needed to talk to you, Charlie. The other day, I wasn't completely honest with you. About the lawyer."

She paused, and I closed my eyes. I leaned against the wall of the hallway. "It's okay, Mom."

"No, it's not okay. I lied to you, Charlie. And I told myself I would never lie to you."

"I know what's going on. You're seeing that guy. The lawyer."

The other end of the line fell silent for a few seconds before Mom replied. "You know?"

"I, uh, yeah—I found out about it." I wasn't going to tell my mom that I'd been stalking her. No, not stalking. Just following in a healthy way. I paused and took a breath. "You know what, Mom? I'm not mad that you didn't tell me."

"You're not?"

"No. I get it. This is different. For both of us. Is he the first guy you've dated since… since Dad died?"

"He is," Mom admitted. "And I was worried about it. For a long time, I never thought I'd find anyone else. I never wanted to find anyone else. I had your father, and we had twenty-two glorious years together. I couldn't have asked for anything else. He was the love of my life. And that's all I really needed. I knew what I had, and I enjoyed it, and I grieved when he died, but I never felt the urge to look for it again."

I blinked back the tears that threatened to overwhelm me. Dad really had been the greatest.

A pause ensued, and instead of chiming in, I gave Mom the time she needed to get her thoughts in order.

"And then I met Lucas. He was hired by my work when we needed some contracts done with a new vendor. He was nice. Friendly. He's a widower as well; his wife died in a swimming accident eight years ago. We bonded over that and decided to go out, and the next thing I know, I'm seeing him again. And again. I knew I had to tell you. I just…"

"Didn't know how I was going to react?" I finished.

"Well, yes. I love you, Charlie, but you can be a little bit unpredictable."

I laughed, hoping I sounded natural. "Don't worry, Mom. What did you think I was going to do, stalk you?"

"No, of course not. Don't be ridiculous. Only someone certifiable would do that to their own mother. But you know. I worried about what you would think."

"It's all good, Mom," I said. "I get it. I'm happy for you."

"When you saw me the other day, I panicked. I didn't want you to know yet. We're not all that serious. But the fact that I lied nagged at me. You deserve to know the truth. You're an adult. I don't have to hide this sort of thing from you."

"Thanks, Mom. I appreciate it. And don't worry. I'm okay. You don't have to think about me when you do these sorts of things."

"Of course I do. You're my daughter. The fact that you're grown doesn't change that."

"I love you, Mom."

"I love you, too, Charlie."

My phone buzzed just then, and I pulled it from my ear for a moment to see who was calling. It was Zoe. Weird that she didn't text.

I ignored her call; I could get back to her later.

"If you're happy, Mom, I'm happy. Seriously. I know that's what Dad would have wanted for you too."

Mom let out a chuckle. "Oh, he most certainly would have. You know, back in the day, when we were young and a bit sprightlier, he suggested that we could have—"

"Okay, and you're not going to finish that sentence," I interrupted.

My phone buzzed again. Zoe, again.

"Listen Mom, I have to go, okay? Zoe keeps calling."

"All right, all right, I can take the hint."

"No, seriously. She's actually calling. I'll talk to you soon, okay? Thanks for telling me. I appreciate it."

"Say hello from me."

I switched over to the call from Zoe. "Hey, what's up?"

"I'm in the ER. Get over here now. Jake's been shot."

Chapter 23

My heart plummeted to the floor, through the ground and sank into the core of the earth.

"What?"

"He just came in. I have to go. He's getting prepped for surgery. I don't have details, just get over here now."

I didn't remember ending the call. I didn't remember leaving the resort and jumping into Queenie. I didn't remember pulling out into traffic or driving to the hospital, but it must have happened because the next thing I remembered was running through the doors of the ER, feeling like I was going to throw up.

About half a dozen cops were roaming around the waiting area.

Jake. Jake had been shot. He was in surgery. Was he going to make it? Was he going to die? What was I going to do if he died? I couldn't think about that.

I ran up to the desk, which Cora manned.

"Jake," I managed to say, my fingers clutching at the edge of the desk, desperate for something to hold on to. "He's here. Is he okay? Is he dead?"

Cora immediately went into nurse mode. "Charlie, look at me. He's in surgery. The doctors are taking the best care of him they can. Zoe wanted me to bring you to her as soon as you got here. Come on. We're going to go see her."

Cora got up and led me down the hall.

"Is he going to die?" I asked, terrified of the answer but equally terrified of not knowing.

"I'm going to be honest. I don't know," Cora replied. "But I will tell you this: he's got the best chance of making a recovery here."

As we walked down the hall, memories came flooding back to me. My dad's last illness. Walking through these walls like they were a liminal space. Existing but not existing. Feeling like the world was crumbling around me.

Dad dying here, in his hospital bed, surrounded by beeping machines, beige walls, and family who loved him. The day my world collapsed. The day it changed forever.

I couldn't go through this again.

Cora led me into a small staff room, and the next thing I knew, Zoe had wrapped her arms around me. "Oh, Charlie," she muttered into my ear. "He's in surgery."

I couldn't hold it in any longer. I began bawling

my eyes out, crying into Zoe's shoulder as she held me close. "I can't do this, Zoe. I can't. Is he going to be okay? What happened?"

"Liam says they were arresting a suspect in a string of robberies. The man appeared to be cooperating, then at the last second, he pulled out a gun and fired. Jake tried to get out of the way, but he was shot. Liam shot the man in the shoulder before he could get off a second shot. The bullet just barely nicked his femoral artery, and the surgeons are fixing it now. I got the latest update five minutes ago. It's going well."

At that last sentence, all the strength I had left me. I collapsed onto the floor, and Zoe sat down on it with me, wrapping an arm around my shoulder and pulling me close.

"I'm a doctor. You know I can't tell you he's going to be okay," she said. "There are so many variables. But the odds are in his favor. They really are, Charlie. If anyone's going to pull through from this, it's Jake."

"I just… I can't handle this. I didn't realize what it would mean. How big it would be. Jake puts himself in danger all the time, and now he's in surgery."

"He is."

"I knew he was a cop. I knew he put himself in dangerous situations."

"Knowing something with your rational brain and feeling it happen are two different things," Zoe said softly. "That's normal."

"I didn't realize how much it would feel like when Dad died," I said, my voice barely more than a whisper.

Zoe pressed me close to her. "The difference is Jake is likely going to make it through this. I know it's awful. I know you're hurting. Let it out. Let it hurt, but he's in the best possible hands."

I sobbed on the floor of a random room in the hospital, with Zoe holding me tight, until finally her phone buzzed.

She glanced at the screen. "He's out of surgery. The doctor thinks he's going to be fine."

I was out of energy to cry at that point. So I just sat on the floor and buried my head in my hands. Jake was going to be okay.

Eventually, I got up. "I want to see him."

"You can be in his room, but he likely won't wake up from the anesthetic for a while," Zoe warned.

"I don't care. I just want to see him." I got up, groaning slightly as my bones reminded me I wasn't twenty anymore. I'd been sitting in the same spot for… Well, I wasn't sure how long. Hours? It felt like years.

"I tried calling you again, but you must have been driving. Where's your phone?"

I looked around, feeling my pockets. "I don't know. I don't remember much after you called. I just… I think I just came here as fast as I could."

"Okay. Can I call anyone for you? Your Mom? Dot or Rosie?"

I shook my head. "No. Thanks. I just want to wait for him to wake up. It's fine."

"I'll send a nurse in to take care of you, too, Charlie," Zoe said.

"I'm fine," I insisted.

"You aren't. And that's okay. It's okay not to be fine. Someone you love has just been through something life-threatening."

I scrunched up my face. "I don't *love* him."

Zoe shot me a look. "Whatever you say, Charlie."

She held the door open, and I passed through it. I followed her through the halls of the hospital until we reached the surgery recovery ward. Zoe pulled aside a privacy curtain, and I let out a tiny gasp as I saw Jake lying on the bed in front of me.

He was lying on his side. His eyes were closed, and an IV was hooked up to the top of his hand. A small lock of hair fell across his forehead, and I instinctively wanted to reach over and brush it out of the way. His chest rose and fell in a steady rhythm.

Zoe strode over to the front of the bed and grabbed the chart. She studied it and turned to me with a smile. "Everything looks good here, Charlie. He should be awake any minute now. Want me to stay?"

I shook my head. "Thanks, but I'm sure you have, you know, actual patients and stuff."

Zoe smiled. "My shift ended two hours ago."

"You're truly the best friend ever, do you know that? I love you so much."

"I love you too."

"But seriously, I'll be okay. Go home. It's fine, now that I know he's okay."

She reached over and squeezed my hand. "Okay. If you're sure."

I nodded. "I am. Now that I'm here, that he's here… it's all good. I'll be okay."

"Call me if you need anything. Borrow someone's phone, I guess, since yours is AWOL."

I chuckled slightly. "At least I had a good reason to lose it this time."

"You certainly did."

Zoe left, and I pulled a chair over and sat down next to Jake's bed, facing him. I watched him breathing, in and out, and after about five minutes, he started stirring.

When his eyes opened, a sense of relief I couldn't even begin to describe washed over me.

"Charlie," he muttered, his voice hoarse.

"Jake," I replied, immediately sitting up and grabbing him a cup of water from the nearby stand. I handed the cup to him.

He took it, rolling onto his back with a wince. "What happened?"

"You were shot. You were trying to arrest a guy

for the robberies, and he pulled out a gun. You had surgery. It nicked your femoral."

"Right," Jake replied, drinking the water. "That explains why my ass hurts so much."

"Wait, *that's* where you got shot? In the ass?" The emotions of the last few hours caught up to me, and I began to laugh uncontrollably.

"Hey, I got *shot*," Jake replied, but his face broke into a smile, and before I knew it, he was laughing along with me, despite his complaining. "You can't make fun of me for getting shot in the ass. That's rude."

Tears began flowing from my eyes. "I can't believe I thought you were going to die. You know those cheeks are so thick there was no way a bullet was going to get through them."

"I guess I should take that as a compliment," Jake said.

"You know it is. You got shot in the butt. I'm never going to let you live that down."

"You get Tasered like every week, and you don't hear me making fun of you," Jake shot back.

I buried my head in my hands. "I'm sorry. It's just… Ugh, I thought you were going to die. And you're going to be fine. And you only got shot in the ass."

I lost it again to a fit of giggles, and when I looked up once more, Jake had an amused expression on his face.

"I'm glad this is so funny for you."

"Only because I've spent the past I-don't-know-how-many hours sitting in a room with Zoe, crying my eyes out," I admitted.

"I was scared too," Jake said quietly. "There was a lot of blood. I wasn't sure I was going to make it."

"Being here, seeing this, it reminded me of my dad," I said. "His last illness. Being in the hospital when he died. I'm glad you're not dead."

"So am I."

"I'm never going to let you live down the fact that you got shot in the butt."

"Almost died in the line of duty," Jake corrected.

"Can you imagine if you had? How embarrassing that would have been? I'd have told everyone at your funeral too."

Jake laughed. "I don't doubt it."

I shoved him over slightly and lay down in the bed next to him. Jake wrapped an arm around me.

"It's nice to know you care this much about me," he teased.

"If you died, who else would I spend my whole day annoying?" I replied.

I hadn't handled it well, thinking there was a chance he was going to die. Seeing him injured in the line of duty. I hadn't handled it well at all.

Was this what life would be like with Jake, in the future? Feeling like this? Was it going to happen again? Or worse?

As much as I laughed at the fact that he'd been shot in the ass, I was scared out of my wits.

We always spoke about Jake's worries that I was going to get hurt, but I'd never factored in how I would react if Jake got hurt.

Could I handle this?

"What are you thinking about?" Jake murmured.

"How you got shot in the butt," I replied with a grin.

"No, really. I can tell from the look on your face. It's more serious than that."

I sighed. "I never thought about how it would feel if *you* were the one who got hurt. And I don't know if I can handle it."

Jake reached down and grabbed my hand. "It's hard."

"It is. I mean, you're okay. I don't want you to die. I like annoying you. And I don't want to ever feel like I did today again."

"I'm not reckless. It was out of the blue. I couldn't have done anything differently."

"I know. But that doesn't change how I felt. I have no memory of driving here. I just remember Zoe telling me you were shot, and the next thing I knew, I was in the hospital. How do I go through every day, knowing that I could feel like this again? Go through this again? Or, worse."

"I'd give you an answer if I could. But I can't, because I know exactly how you feel. I'm terrified, every single day. You know that."

"I do. But why do you do it?"

"Because the alternative is not having you in my life at all. And as much as it hurts when I see you throw yourself into a dangerous situation, as much as I feel like you've taken ten years off my life already, and while I'll be tempted to charge you for blood pressure medications the day my doctor says I need them, it'll be worth it. I'd rather be scared shitless with you than living a stress-free life without you. And I guess you need to decide if I'm worth the same to you."

A silence hung in the air between us.

I stared up at the ceiling. "Jake?"

"Yeah?"

"I think I love you." I'd never said those words to a man before. And yet, they were true. I really did. I couldn't hide from it. No one reacted the way I did today if they didn't really, truly love someone.

"I love you, too, Charlie."

"You're worth it. I want to be with you. Even when you get shot in the ass."

Jake buried his face in my hair to hide his laugh. "Excuse me, I'm a hero."

"I hope they let me make a speech at the ceremony where you pick up your commendation."

"You're impossible."

"And yet you love me."

"I do," Jake admitted.

"I love you too."

I spent another hour or so with Jake. Doctors and nurses took their turns coming in. One checked me out for shock and determined I was fine but didn't take it well when I asked if I could have some morphine just in case.

"I guess I'll go," I said. "Going by how many cops were in the waiting room when I came in, half the Maui PD is out there waiting to see how you're doing. And I guess Liam is probably one of them."

Jake smiled. "You wish he got shot instead, don't you?"

"I wish for that to happen every day."

"He might have saved my life. If he hadn't reacted as quickly as he did, who knows what would have happened?" Jake said.

"Fine. I guess he gets a bit of credit for that. But he's still a potato with a gun. I'll leave for a bit, though. You still owe me dinner. And all the cocktails I want at MonkeyPod."

Jake chuckled. "How could I forget?"

"Don't think getting yourself shot is going to get you out of this."

"Wouldn't dream of it."

"I'll come back later to see you. Do you want me to sneak you in any outside food?"

Jake shook his head. "I'm not really hungry right now. Must be the drugs."

I gave him a kiss, thinking how grateful I was that he was still here. "Okay. Text me if you change your mind. I'm going to see if I can find my phone somewhere."

"Have fun."

"And Jake?"

"Yeah?"

"I'm glad you're okay."

He cracked a small smile. "Me too."

I left the room, pausing for one more second to get another look at him before I left. Jake was okay. He was safe. He was going to be fine.

We were going to be fine.

He was right. Today had been awful. I wasn't sure I could handle feeling like this again. But excruciating pain from time to time was so much better than a lifetime without him. I would just have to handle the fact that he did a dangerous job, the same way he did with me.

I stepped back outside and realized I had no idea what time it was. Inside the windowless rooms of the hospital, time meant nothing. But as I emerged, I realized night had fallen. Stars twinkled above, competing with the bright lights of Kahului.

I headed toward Queenie, pulling my keys out of my pocket. I breathed in the night air as I let it relax me.

Suddenly, pain seared through the small of my back. I let out a cry as I fell to the ground. I knew what this was. Someone had just Tasered me.

"What the hell? You said she was going to pass

out," someone's voice said above me. "She's still conscious."

"That's weird. Every time I've Tasered someone, they've been knocked out for a second. Whatever. Come on. Let's get her in the car."

I tried to scream, but no sound came out. I kicked and flailed and heard one of the men shout as I connected.

"Shut the fuck up, man."

"She kicked me in the kneecap."

"We have to get her out of here. Come on. I'll Tase her again."

Pain coursed through me once more, and the next thing I knew, a cloth was being shoved into my mouth. I kicked and struggled as much as I could, but it was no use. The two men had me.

They picked me up, carried me to the trunk of the car parked next to Queenie, and shoved me inside the small space.

I looked up at them, unable to make out more than silhouettes in the dark. But one of them was grinning, his white teeth catching the small bit of light emanating from inside the trunk.

"The Ham brothers are really looking forward to this reunion," he said before slamming the trunk shut.

This wasn't good.

Book 9 - Turtle Terror: With the Ham brothers trying to get their revenge on Charlie, she's not about to sit back and let them ruin her life.

But while she's trying to stop them, there are other problems on the island. A woman Dot knows has been killed, and she wants justice. Obviously, Charlie is on the case. But will the crew be able to keep Rosie and Dot's true skills secret from those close to them?

And how is Jake going to handle both his recovery from his gunshot wound, and help bring the Seattle gang to justice?

As Charlie gets closer to the island's killer, she realizes there's more to this crime than she first thought, and she's in more danger than she expected. Will Charlie get to the bottom of this case before she becomes turtle food?

Click here to pre-order Turtle Terror now. (coming November, 2023)

About the Author

Jasmine Webb is a thirty-something who lives in the mountains most of the year, dreaming of the beach. When she's not writing stories you can find her chasing her old dog around, hiking up moderately-sized hills, or playing Pokemon Go.

Want to find out how Dot and Rosie met? Sign up for Jasmine's newsletter to get that story, and be the first to find out about new releases here: http://www.authorjasminewebb.com/newsletter

You can also connect with her on other social media:

Also by Jasmine Webb

Charlotte Gibson Mysteries

Aloha Alibi

Maui Murder

Beachside Bullet

Pina Colada Poison

Hibiscus Homicide

Kalikimaka Killer

Surfboard Stabbing

Mai Tai Massacre

Turtle Terror (coming November 2023)

Poppy Perkins Mysteries

Booked for Murder

Read Between the Lies

On the Slayed Page

Put Pen to Perpetrator (coming August 2023)

Mackenzie Owens Mysteries

Dead to Rights (coming September 2023)

Against the Odds (coming September 2023)

Made in United States
Orlando, FL
23 January 2024

42848481R00174